Someone Else's Shoes

A collection of short stories and monologues

Pat White

*All proceeds from the sale of this book
will be donated to Sir Michael Sobell House.*

Someone Else's Shoes

ISBN 0-9552451-0-9
ISBN 978-0-9552451-0-7

Published by PJ Publishing, Oxford.
First published in 2006.

Designed by Oxford Medical Illustration
A department of The Oxford Radcliffe Hospitals NHS Trust.

Printed and bound by Parchment the Printers, Cowley, Oxford.

For Joan May Field

She would have loved this

Acknowledgements

Many, many thanks are due to the following people.

Ian Laing, High Sheriff of Oxfordshire, whose generous support and sponsorship of this book has allowed the proceeds from every sale to be donated in full to Sir Michael Sobell House.

Neil Drury for his gift of the beautiful cover.

Joanne Harris and Seraphina Clarke Limited, for granting permission to include 'Dryad' in this collection.

Colin Dexter, for prompting 'Margaret Ashley's Memory'.

The writers of Oxford Voices, especially Tess Boswood, for encouragement and expertise. They really know their stuff.

Barbara Firth, for tirelessly reviewing everything I've ever written.

Megan Turmezei, for dedicated quality assurance.

Adrian Sutton, my greatest fan, and owner of the boot.

And everyone involved in the production of the book, for making it a painless process.

Someone Else's Shoes

A collection of short stories and monologues.

Contents

Foreword

Pat White was an Executive Director of the Oxford Radcliffe Hospitals NHS Trust from 1991 to 1999, with responsibility for Planning and Performance Management. In that role, she and her team supported Sobell House in bids for additional funding, improved equipment and facilities. She was also one of a number of Directors charged with reviewing us and our work. As a result, she came to understand the pressures and frustrations we faced, as well as the excellent services we provide. She has offered the proceeds of her book of short stories to support the work of Sir Michael Sobell House.

Sir Michael Sobell House is based in the grounds of the Churchill Hospital, Oxford. The contemporary hospice, also now called a palliative care service, exists to help look after patients facing a life threatening illness, for example, cancer, heart failure or degenerative neurological disease. Our service covers most of Oxfordshire, a population of over half a million people. Besides the 20 bed inpatient ward at Sobell House we have a large team of community nurses seeing people in their own homes and a hospital team seeing inpatients in the Oxford Hospitals, and particularly in the John Radcliffe and the Radcliffe Infirmary.

The Hospice was opened in April 1976 by HRH the Duchess of Kent. The Friends of Sobell House, later to become the Sobell House Hospice Charity, had been established two years earlier to raise funds. The Hospice was built by a personal donation from Sir Michael Sobell, when he was President of the National Society for Cancer Relief (now Macmillan) and money raised from the community. There was agreement that the NHS would continue to provide the annual revenue thereafter.

In the early nineties, Sobell House faced the same financial pressures as much of the Health Service, and had to consider closing four beds. However, the Charity stepped in and committed £100,000 to ensure that we could continue to offer 20 beds. Palliative care has been described as 'low tech and high touch' which means in practice that most of the budget pays for staff.

Over the last 15 years, recognition of palliative care services, and demand for them, has grown significantly. Our ability to keep up with this demand has been helped enormously by a continually increasing annual grant from Sobell House Hospice Charity. In 2005 they donated £825,000 - roughly one third of our annual budget. The Charity also raised nearly £4 million in 2001 to re-build the Hospice.

The production costs of the book have been met by Ian Laing, High Sheriff of Oxfordshire and former Non Executive Director of the Trust, through whose generosity all money raised from sales will go directly to the Charity.

We are delighted to receive Pat's gift of this collection of short stories. We have enjoyed reading them, and hope you will too.

Michael Minton, *Medical Director*
Sir Michael Sobell House

One for the Ladies

"I'm gonna sit right down and write myself a letter."

Frank announces his entrance as usual with a song, comes through the double doors and captivates his audience immediately with his baritone. "C'mon now ladies, who made this one famous?"

Peg wedges open the sluice room door, the better to enjoy the performance. "Twenty past nine on the dot, we could set clocks by him." She smiles in anticipation.

So do the ladies.

"It's glad I am to see you looking so well on this beautiful mornin'. I hope you're ready for your tea now?" He pushes the gleaming trolley towards the first bed, parks it deftly at the end and pours from the big chrome pot.

"And make–believe it came from you."

He croons to Alice, standing smartly beside her bed. "Plenty of milk and two sugars."

Alice is ready. Today she wears a pink chenille bed jacket and looks in the peak of health.

"Would that be a touch of lipstick ya have on?"

She takes the cup and smiles up at him coquettishly. "Perhaps."

"Well it's very becomin', if I might make so bold."

"Why thank you Frank." She fluffs up her hair. "Now, was it Perry Como?"

"Ah Alice, I thought this one might catch ya out." He moves down the ward ready to pour another cup.

"I'm gonna write words oh so sweet,"

"You are, are yer? My Eddie catches sight of 'em an' 'e'll be after you Frank O'Brien, that's for sure." Emily looks stern, rather like the queen with steel grey hair teased into cream horns at her temples, but she prods him playfully in the ribs.

"And here's me thinkin' 'tis love we have. Now would ya look at that, Emily. Wait while I get a fresh saucer."

"Good morning Mr O'Brien. In trouble already I see." Sister Johnson grins from behind her desk.

"Good mornin' to you Sister. And if you don't mind me sayin' 'tis these ladies of yours givin' me the trouble. They're terrible wicked to a poor workin' man. Now, will ya take a cup yourself?"

"Not yet, thanks. I'm off to speak to Peg. I'll have some later."

"They're gonna knock me off my feet."

"Frank Sinatra?" she offers.

"Indeed, Sister, it was not."

"He's in fine voice this morning." Sister Johnson joins

Peg in the sluice room. "I don't know how he does it."

"What, get away with his teasing? Frank didn't kiss the Blarney Stone, he swallowed it whole."

Sister laughs. "That I can believe."

"Besides, it's not disrespect, it's real affection he feels for them."

"I know Peg, and so do they. He does them the power of good. But what I meant was how does he carry the tune with all those interruptions? Just seems to pick up right where he left off."

"Don't ask me, I can't sing a note. But he's always been a good singer. Could've been professional, and likes nothing more than a good audience." Peg opens the steriliser. "Anyone going home today?"

"Just Mrs Ellison. Would you help her get ready and make sure she's got all her bits and bobs? The ambulance will be here at about half past two. That gives her plenty of time for lunch, and to say her good–byes. I expect there'll be tears. She always has a little weep even though she's back every fortnight."

"It can't be much fun for her in that big house, hardly any visitors except the Social Services. How she gets up the stairs I'll never know. She won't sleep downstairs though, says it's not proper. My Mum was like that. Took her half an hour sometimes to get up to the bedroom. She'd have a right old moan about it but she wouldn't give in. We moved her in with us in the end. We had a flat then so there weren't any stairs. Couldn't complain then could she? Mind you, she found plenty else to keep us on our toes – right up till she died. Game old bird she was." Peg smiles, lost in thought for a moment. "You know that Frank does the meals–on–wheels run at the weekends. Well, he's going to have a word with Mrs Ellison before she goes, see if he can't persuade her."

"That would make such a difference. He's got a heart of gold, that man." She moves to the doorway and chuckles. "And what a flirt! Mind you, I think he might've met his match here."

Frank stops by Vera's bed.

"A lot of kisses on the bottom,"

Shrieks can be heard from the ward.

Peg laughs as she reaches for the next bedpan. "Now there's a thought to conjure with."

Sister stifles her own giggles as she heads back to her desk.

"Now, now ladies," Frank feigns shock. "What kind of a way is that to behave? And me the poor innocent. Here's your tea, Vera, strong and hot."

She sets down her newspaper and peers over her glasses, one eyebrow raised. "Just like you luv."

"You'll have me blushin', sure ya will," But he flexes his biceps as he walks away, and gets a whistle or two.

"I'll be glad I got 'em."

Frank stops. He looks across the ward and tiptoes to the head of the next bed. Kneeling down to be close, he gently takes one of Maud's pale hands in his and whispers....

"I'm gonna smile and say I hope you're feeling better."

Her eyelids flicker open. Watery eyes struggle to focus and she gives him the hint of a smile.

"There now me darlin' how are ya today?"

A slight shake of her head.

"Ah not so good." He stokes her hand. "You'll not be wantin' tea then."

Her eyes close.

"I'll tell ya what we'll do. You rest now while I take these good ladies their tea. Then I'll be back with a fresh pot and we'll drink it together. How would that be me lovely?"

But Maud has already slipped back into sleep.

Sister puts a hand on Frank's shoulder and nods kindly, sharing his concern. She takes Maud's wrist.

"It's a good strong pulse for such a frail old girl. She could surprise us yet, you know."

He moves back to his trolley, "I hope so, Sister, that I do." and busies himself with cups and things till he's ready to go on.

"And close with love the way you do."

"What'll you have this mornin' Marjorie, tea or coffee?"

"Some of that love you're singing about'll do for me Francis." No bed jacket for Marjorie. She's in blue–flowered winceyette buttoned firmly to the neck. "And don't you be fooled by the floral flannel, 'cos there's life in this old girl yet." She tilts her chin at him.

"And what about my good lady wife? Would you make a dishonest man of me Marjorie Simkin?"

"I just might. Go on then, spoilsport, give us a coffee." She winks as she takes it. "And my money's on Dean Martin."

"It is, is it? And if I were a bettin' man I'd take you on – and I'd be the richer."

"I'm gonna sit right down and write myself a letter,"
"So you're off home today Pauline. Perhaps it's a letter from you I'll be gettin'?"

"Gladly dear, but I'll be back 'ere like as not 'fore you gets time to read it. 'Ello Peg, luv, 'ave you come to get us up?"

"I have, Mrs Ellison, but not till you've finished your tea. Just you take your time. In fact, I think I'll join you if this old Romeo can spare a cup."

"That I can me darlin'," he says sweetly and drops to one knee, hands clasped over his heart.

"and make believe it came from you."
"Will ya not give me a kiss and make me day." All eyes turn to Peg.

"I will not you ol' devil, get up off your knees." Then, with a twinkle in her eye, "You'll just have to wait till we get home."

This gets a round of applause.

"You're a hard woman Peggy O'Brien, didn't I always say so."

"Me, hard? Soft as butter more like." Peg leans towards him and whispers "Now don't you fret love, I'll keep an eye on your Aunt Maud and come and get you if there's a need to." She relents and gives him a kiss on the cheek.

Frank gives her arm a gentle squeeze, blinks away a tear and turns back to his ladies. "There now, wouldn't ya just know she couldn't resist? And it was Fats Waller," he calls as he heads for the doors. "So who'll join me in a chorus before I go on me way?"

The Last Train

It's a year to the day and the first time I've come. This is not a place to spend a birthday. The hospital was part of our lives for so long and, afterwards, I needed to adjust. But at last I can accept all that happened.

Today the early morning mist is thick. The damp from the grass soaks through my shoes but I hardly notice, or care. I wander among the sentried markers reading a name, a date, a message. I'm in no hurry.

I know where to find the grave. Not row and column number, nothing so impersonal, but by the magnificent copper beech. I'll see it soon enough.

Saturday July 17th 1971, 10 am. Twin girls born to Celia and Thomas Webberly at the local general hospital are healthy, happy and in very fine voice. I, Charlotte the firstborn, beat my sister Nina into the world by eleven minutes and set the pattern for the future. Nina, responding to the challenge, is first with everything else – childhood ailments, trips abroad, graduation – but I don't seem to mind.

We are not identical. No single egg divides in our

creation. Two eggs, vying for position even then perhaps. Nor are we alike. I'd think it strange to find we were. We share our parents and a childhood home but not much more. Except, that is, our mother's flame red hair, and a strangely curved nail on the little finger of our left hand. An odd feature I always think.

Wednesday July 18th 2001, 9 am and the sun is already warm. The fields and trees look newly washed after yesterday's downpour. The embankment is steep and smothered in summer flowers. Smells mingle – warm grass, cow parsley, meadowsweet, red clover. They soothe and mark the season. My focus is sharp and clear in the yellow light, unlike my head. A little too much birthday wine, or lack of sleep, have left a fuzz which I hope the walk will help dispel before I have to drive home. Our mother's Springer Spaniel is an eager yet undemanding companion.

As I pass through the low brick tunnel which links east and west pastures, the small stone church, unused but not unconsecrated, comes into view. It sits beside the railway line which runs from London to the north west but with no station close enough to serve a congregation. I used to imagine the villagers and farmhands arriving on horseback or on foot along paths which cannot now be seen, trampled by generations of grazing sheep. I know the door will be unlocked but won't go in.

I remember that as children we believe the church is haunted, with good reason. On December 24th, 1874 the 10 o'clock train from Paddington was derailed just here, cause unknown. It is said that the vicar and his vergers were preparing for midnight mass. They knew at once the meaning of the awful noise and, horrified by what they saw, rang the church bell to raise the alarm. The dead and injured were brought into the church and tended there. For that day, and much of the next, the grim task of identification overshadowed the village. Prayers of a different sort were offered up that Christmas.

In our girlish way we know if we go in we'll see them. Though I don't admit it, I'm not certain how they might appear but floating images of white, dark holes for eyes, and ghastly moaning come to mind. On rainy afternoons we dare ourselves, and one another. Then one day Nina stands in the porch and, with a hand on the plaited iron ring, looks back at me.

"Aren't you coming?" She twists the ring and the latch lifts.

I can't reply. My tongue is stuck in a mouth so dry no effort will release it. My knees begin to buckle and I grab the bench for something solid to hang on to. I make no move towards her. Nina shrugs, walks through the door and it swings shut behind her.

For hours it seems I wait while the rain makes dark red strings of my hair and sticks it to my head. When she reappears I rush to meet her, questions ready.

Her lips are shut, clamped tight to form a thin white line, her freckles vivid contrast to the pallor of her skin. We hurry home in silence.

The sun is hotter now and I am glad to enter the wood. A line of hazels, coppiced into living fans, provides some shade. I wander along the avenue formed between the trees and embankment listening to the sounds of summer. The larks, so high they are out of sight, trill their crystal song. A pheasant startles me from somewhere in the wood with its harsh creak of a cry. I hear the raucous, two–tone klaxon as the train approaches and check the time. Almost 10, I need to head back.

I turn, about to call the dog, when noise engulfs me. A scream of tearing metal. The rhythm of the wheels is amplified to deafen as they ride the sleepers not the track. The engine and carriages are thrown into a dreadful dance. Huge concrete slabs are torn up and scattered, light as matchsticks. The track unpeels, becomes a deadly whip. I stand and stare, my own scream fighting for release. I know she's on that train.

Finally it comes to rest, a broken–backed thing, the bones of which are tossed on both sides of the track. I find myself entangled, held, without the strength or will to move. The silence surprises me. So does the cold. When I see them I battle to accept what I can see. There will be an explanation but I'm much too tired for reason.

There are tens of them, moving through the wreckage. Grey, they're all in grey. At first I think some sort of safety wear, protection against fire. Then gradually, as they come closer, their clothing becomes clearer. Gentlemen in long frock coats, top hats askew; high–waisted ladies wrapped in shawls, bonnets tied securely, button boots. Winter clothes which ought to be a hindrance but are not, their progress swift and sure. They guide those who are able, gently lift and carry those with injuries more severe. They work together tirelessly, know exactly what to do. I try to move, to struggle to my feet and when a cool hand reaches out to touch my brow I slide, gratefully, into the welcome dark.

They were excellent in the hospital, trained and professional. Nina was the doctors' prime concern, the focus of their expertise. It seemed the nurses feared more for our mother, while my presence demanded no attention. They brought her tea, of course, and tried to tempt with food. But she had no appetite, except for news. And that was hard to comprehend. Just two fatalities the papers said, though some of the injured remain critical. No–one has been able to explain how so many could escape, even those who were badly hurt. A miracle they called it.

I sat with Nina, willing her to sense that I was there. She was so pale, and still. Linked by tubes and wires to grey machines which drew their life from her then proved they had on flat black screens. Our mother drifted in and out, unable to settle, looking for a sign but finding none. She despaired, could not respond to my attempts to soothe.

I stayed with Nina all the while and held her hand, cradling her palm. I stroked her wrist for warmth, unsure which of us was colder. One day I ran my thumb across that crooked nail and there it was......a squeeze. She did respond, I'm sure she did.

It's a year to the day and the first time I've come yet I know where to find the grave. Not row and column number, nothing so impersonal, but by the magnificent copper beech. I see it now the mist has cleared. The morning sun, still low, sets the tree aflame. Its dark red leaves glint in the light and drip necklaces of rainbow jewels. I stand beneath holding out my hands to catch them, watch them slipping through my fingers while I wait. And then I see her. She stands behind the headstone, back towards me but I know it's her. Faded strands of once–red hair curl at the nape of her neck. I join her and we move together to the foot of the grave. We kneel in silence, lost in separate worlds. She takes her time to rearrange the flowers.

She has aged. She's thinner now. I note the hollow cheeks, and the dark half–moons beneath her eyes. I marvel that the shock which stole the colour from her hair has spared her brows, giving her a strangely painted look.

I kiss her. She finishes the flowers, turns to me as if to speak but settles for the briefest smile, which I return. I stand, look down upon her, say good–bye. Then, loth to leave I watch her lean across and, with a crooked nail, begin to trace the polished letters on my grave.

Angels in Trousers

The girl sits on an upturned wooden crate, a cushion for protection against splinters. Her colouring book is open on her lap and, with tongue peeping to aid concentration and meticulous pencil strokes, she gives Snow White a crimson skirt.

The boy lies sideways on the camp bed with his legs up the wall of the shelter. He runs the toe of one slipper up and down the ridged metal, the beam of his torch searching the curved roof for spiders. His score so far is twelve, which is low. More disappointingly, none is big enough to scare his sister before scurrying back into the dark.

"Is Dad dead then?" The boy switches off his torch.

"Course not, silly."

"So how can he have wings? You don't get wings till you die, we learned that in Sunday School. You get wings and a long white frock. Then you float about in heaven or sit at the Right Hand of God. Reverend Hooper told us."

"Well, he's not dead. He's coming home this weekend isn't he?"

"Then I bet he won't have wings."

"He will too. I heard Mum say when she was on the telephone to Grandad. She told him Dad had got his Stripes and his Wings. It was at a Passing Out Parade."

"What's that?"

"I'm not quite sure but I think it's when you fall over. Remember when Uncle Brian was digging the hole for our shelter and it was very hot but he kept digging because he wanted to get it finished?"

"Yes."

"Then he went all funny and fell over. Well, Mum said he'd passed out."

Philip considers this for a moment. "So was Dad digging a hole?"

"I don't think so. But I expect having wings fixed on would make him hot. Perhaps that's why he passed out."

"Come on you two, it's time you went to sleep." Anne comes across from her chair by the door. "Move over Philip and let Amy get in beside you. That's it, snuggle down." She pulls the rough grey blankets up to their chins and gives each a kiss. "Night night, loves, sleep tight."

"Night night Mum."

"Mum?"

"Yes Amy."

"Dad is coming home on Friday isn't he?"

"Of course love. He wouldn't miss seeing you two for anything. Now try to get some sleep." She checks the guard around the paraffin heater and turns down the wick.

The shelter is in their back garden. Their Dad had made sure they had one, for the times when they couldn't get to the underground station, Amy and Philip love it. Amy likes to imagine she's in a faraway place. Sometimes, when she closes her eyes and smells that oily paraffin smell, she's on a boat sailing off to find her Dad.

Philip comes here often. He has important things hidden in secret places and must check that all is in order. He's the man of the house now and intends to be ready.

"Are they all right?" Josie drops her knitting into her lap.

"Seem to be. They still treat this as an adventure." Anne takes a cigarette from her pack then offers it to her friend.

"Just as well." They both light up. "It wouldn't do to have them frightened. Ssh, listen........."

The women wait, heads cocked, for the engine to stop. They track its path overhead. The Doodlebug continues out of earshot. Anne knocks on wood, then relaxes.

"Some poor devil's in for it." Josie uncrosses her fingers. "You should really think about sending them away."

"I know, I know. But they've got so much to put up with – the blackout, no school – most of their friends have already gone."

"Well there you are." Josie pats her friend's hand. "And for good reason. We might not always be lucky."

"I'll talk to Bill at the weekend, see what he says." Anne stubs out her cigarette and watches as the mantle on the Tilley Lamp dims. "Do you want more light? I can prime the other lamp."

"No thanks, I think I'll give the knitting a rest. Brian says he's got enough scarves thank you very much."

Anne laughs. "I'm sure Bill would like it, he says Canada's freezing."

"Is he still in Manitoba?"

"No Winnipeg and he'll be......." The siren interrupts her.

Amy is drifting into sleep watching the pattern of stars thrown on to the ceiling by the heater. Wingy–peg. Now she knows it's true.

Next morning Amy announces her plan as she drips the honey Dad brought home onto her bread. "We'll ask Mum if we can look at the photos. Wings are bound to show up."

"D'you think she'll let us?" Philip rebuilds the moat around his porridge castle.

"Let you do what?" Anne comes in from the garden with arms full of washing. "Looks like mischief afoot to me."

"Can we look at the albums Mum? It's too wet to go out and we'll be really, really careful. Please Mum."

Anne smiles at their eagerness. "All right, but

remember to put them back when you've finished. I don't want to find them all over the floor. Erm, just a minute, young man, isn't it your turn to do the dishes?" Philip looks disappointed.

"I'll help."

"Definitely mischief." Anne begins to sort the washing.

Amy turns the little silver key and opens the sideboard door. The familiar smell of varnish and musty wood wafts out. She lifts the first album, spreads it on the floor then lies on her stomach next to her brother.

"What are we looking for?" Philip gently turns a page. "There's Mum and Dad in the garden and one of Dad fixing the car."

"I'm not sure." They're on the third album now and Amy is beginning to doubt. "Although suppose his wings are folded up. That's it they must be, or we'd have seen them before." Enthusiasm revived they reach for number four.

"See, there!" Amy pokes the page, jubilant.

Philip stares at the photo. "Where?" He isn't convinced. He sees Bill climbing into a plane, one foot on the step, parachute strapped in place.

"There. That's where they are. Folded up in that bag. Otherwise they'd be in the way or might even get broken." Determined now, they rush off in search of further proof.

Anne stoops to pick up the album left open on the carpet. She sits, looks at the face smiling back at her with a smile that reaches the camera but not his eyes. She studies the fuselage noticing for the first time the line of black circles and shudders as she identifies bullet holes. She sees Bill's gloved hand grasping the edge of the wing and imagines a white–knuckled fist inside. Her tears dampen the page.

They wait in the dark, eager for the game to begin. From their hiding place under the stairs they'll know just when he arrives.

"Ssh, here he comes." The key's in the lock and Amy clamps a hand over her mouth to contain her excitement, butterflies beating deliciously against her ribs.

"Ready or not, here I come." The familiar voice at last. They tremble as he goes into the parlour and turns on the light. "Now let me see.....anyone behind the sofa? No. Under the sideboard? No. Definitely no–one in here."

They squeeze their eyes shut as the latch clicks, not daring to watch as he passes by. He pauses, ear pressed to the kitchen door then eases it open. "Gotcha!" and he spins on his heel ready to pounce, his arms upraised in the shaft of light, battledress jacket hanging loose.

The children gasp. There are his wings.

Bill collapses onto the sofa and kisses Anne's cheek. "They want you to tuck them in."

"Got them in bed at last, have you?" she teases "They haven't been this excited in a long while."

"And energetic too. They've been jumping all over me, nearly had the shirt off my back."

Anne laughs, "They're just happy to have you home." and heads up the stairs.

"Lights out now, it's getting late." As she kisses Philip she hears the low drone of planes overhead.

"Good luck boys," she calls up to them, as she always does. "safe home."

"Mum?"

"Yes Amy."

"Is Dad an Angel?"

She brushes the hair from her daughter's forehead and smiles. "Yes, love. They all are. Angels in trousers."

Margaret Ashley's Memory

The single noteworthy feature of Margaret Ashley, a small, slim 75–year–old spinster, was a pair of intelligent and kindly eyes. The joy of her life was the cinema; the litter that disfigured the streets of her beloved Oxford was her greatest sadness. A timid soul, she'd never had the courage even gently to rebuke an irresponsible dog–owner whose pet was fouling the pavement. But one late summer afternoon, as she stood at her bus–stop after a matinee performance at the ABC Cinema, two teenagers walked nonchalantly past her, one of them taking a last bite from a burger–roll before throwing the remainder, wrapper and all, on to the pavement.

Margaret's fingers curled, she felt the heat rise to her cheeks. She looked away, battling her indecision, daring herself to confront them. When she turned back they'd stopped walking; the boy stood, one arm draped around the girl's shoulders. She leant against him, one thumb busy with her mobile phone, the other hooked into the belt of her low–slung jeans.

Margaret stared again at the mess of meat and polystyrene. The carton seemed to mock her with a toothless sneer, and she made up her mind. Ignoring the knot tightening in her stomach, she took a deep breath and called after them, as firmly as she could.

"I think you dropped this." Margaret pointed, her arm trembling.

The boy turned, bony shoulders lifting his T–shirt, the front of his black hair sticking up in a challenge.

"You're joking, right?" he scoffed. His eyes narrowed as he came towards her.

She'd been going tell him no, she was not, but the blow took her by surprise, knocked the breath out of her. She reached out to stop herself falling, but couldn't. Her hip struck the pavement with a sickening crack. She lay still in an effort to fend off the pain, trying to memorise all that was happening. Then everything went black.

She woke with a start to the sound of voices. In the past few days she'd grown used to the hospital routine, and particularly enjoyed the lull after lunch. She must have dozed off while waiting. She hadn't meant to; she'd wanted all her wits about her when the policeman arrived, and certainly didn't want him to think her discourteous.

But Constable Benson was understanding, and concerned not to tire her. She was feeling much better, she told him. The operation had been a success. Once the pain in her hip was under control, she hoped to go home.

He'd come to tell her what they'd worked out, from the witness statement and CCTV. Not the whole story, he was sorry to say, and was hoping Margaret could fill in the gaps.

The driver had noticed the youth first, sprawled against the wall, blood running down his face. He'd had more of a shock when he'd seen Margaret, unconscious on the pavement, the contents of her handbag spilled all around. He'd checked she was breathing then phoned for an ambulance and the police.

The CCTV wasn't conclusive but showed a man, about 6 feet tall, chasing after a girl. They wanted to trace him, to help identify her. The lad who'd attacked Margaret was downstairs, in another ward. He wouldn't be going anywhere for a while.

When she heard how badly he'd been injured, Margaret gasped, fingers flying to her mouth.

"Don't you go worrying on his account. It was brave, standing up for yourself like that, though you could have been even more seriously hurt. Still, he got what he deserved."

"No." The force of her words surprised them both. "No," she repeated. "It wasn't him!"

In the silence that followed P. C. Benson studied her. "Are you certain, Miss Ashley? You've had quite a shock."

"I am," she told him, determination hardening her eyes. "It's my mobility I've lost, young man, not my memory."

Her attacker had come from behind, crashing into her, snatching her bag. The skinny youth had rushed to tackle him while Margaret lay helpless on the ground. She'd seen the bigger man punch the youth then lunge for the phone. But the girl was too quick and had sprinted off.

Could she describe him, the constable wondered.

Indeed she could, Margaret had told him.

Close–cropped hair, receding slightly either side of a central peak. His brow rose straight to a well–shaped head. His eyes were slightly hooded, with furrows etched between. But most memorable were the deep curves bracketing his mouth.

"In fact, he looked just like........" Margaret paused, with the hint of a smile. "Bruce Willis. In Diehard 3."

"Diehard 3?" P. C. Benson spluttered.

"Why yes," she told him, a twinkle in her eyes. John McClane was her favourite cop.

Margaret moved slowly to the front door, not yet used to her crutches, and found the young constable on the step. They were following some leads, he'd come to tell her and, thanks to Margaret, expected results. Oh yes, and the two young people waiting in his car would like to come and thank her.

The girl smiled shyly, blond hair falling across one eye. The young man stepped forward, lifting a package. His wound had healed well, Margaret was glad to see, just a faint pink trace against the black of his skin.

While the three of them set to work on the DVD player, Margaret made tea. They soon had it working and stayed to make sure she knew how to use it.

When they'd gone Margaret sifted through the films they'd brought. She found what she wanted, topped up her cup, then settled down to an evening with Bruce.

This story was first entered into the BBC Radio Oxford/ Colin Dexter challenge to complete a story he had begun.

Someone Else's Shoes

"Don't crumple me, it took ages to get like this." Tom stepped back out of my embrace, but not before planting a kiss on the top of my head, and allowed me to study the effect. "What do you think?"

The grey suit was immaculate, emphasising his wide shoulders, the tails just skimming his narrow hips. The plum–coloured cravat was secured discreetly by his father's pearl pin. The plum and grey waistcoat had also once been his father's, but had found a better fit on our son. I looked down quickly as my vision began to blur; I had never seen such highly polished shoes.

Still looking down, I tapped the base of my throat lightly with my finger tips, clearing a non–existent frog, and waited until I could trust my voice.

"Gorgeous, darling. Fabulous. A perfect match for the beautiful bride."

"Cheers Ma." He beamed, blessed me with another kiss then dashed off to join his brother and their friends for breakfast.

I sat at a small table in the bay window, and waited for his father.

"Hi Mum."

I looked up to see Edward, younger son and best man.

"I thought you might need this," he said, pouring me a cup of coffee from a steaming pot. "I did consider something stronger," he laughed, "but it's perhaps a bit early."

"Just a bit, tempting though. Thanks."

"Shall I pour one for Dad?"

"And just how long have you known him?" I checked my watch. "He's probably still asleep."

"Lucky him. Tom was up with the lark." he stifled a yawn. "Got the rest of us up too."

He went off to finish his breakfast. I sipped my coffee, gazing through the window at the river below, meandering along its course.

Tom was three and a half when we met. His mother had died six months earlier from a massive brain haemorrhage. George gave up his job to care for his son. Tom gave up speaking.

They walked into my clinic hand in hand – a small boy in denim trousers, swamped by a sweatshirt with penguins on the front; the man, tall and dishevelled in a baggy jumper and cords. I watched him kneel beside the boy to speak, gently ruffling his hair all the while, then I crossed the room to join them.

"You must be Mr Ellis." I extended my hand. "Jenny Pattison."

"Oh, George, please. Glad to meet you, and this is Tom."

"Hello." I crouched and offered my hand to the boy. He hesitated for a moment, then took it.

"You've come just in time to hear the story. Would you like to sit next to me while I read?"

His father nodded encouragement. "I'll be right here, by the window," he promised. "I'm not going anywhere without you."

For the next few months that was the pattern. George sat in a quiet corner while Tom got to know us. He seemed happy enough, with an eye on his father, but still never uttered a word. The other children accepted his silence without question.

Gradually George ventured further away, always telling Tom when he was going and what time he'd be back. At first, it was just to fetch things from the car. Tom watched from the window. Then George sat in the car to eat his lunch. Tom ate standing in the doorway. But one day he came back to the table. I was delighted. George was ecstatic. We hugged, and Tom smiled.

"Have dinner with us. I'm a passable cook, isn't that right Tom? How about Friday?"

I nodded. "Thanks. I'd love to."

I was sent to the garden with a glass of wine while George and Tom prepared our meal. I stretched out on a recliner, watching the clouds changing their shapes.

"Look at that." I pointed as Tom came to join me. "A big fat elephant gallumphing across the sky."

Tom nodded.

"Whoops, now it's a car with only three wheels."

He laughed.

"Come on, your turn."

He scanned the sky then nudged me to follow a band of cloud streaking towards the pale disc of moon. We watched it transform; a dart, an arrow, a pointed beak trailing feathery wings.

"What is it? A bird?"

He lifted his shoulders and flapped his arms, running along the grass.

"A swan? Of course, that's what it is. A swan dancing with the moon."

After dinner we went back into the garden. The wind had dropped leaving a clear sky, sliding into twilight. George and Tom lay back, sharing a recliner. I kicked off my shoes and stretched out on mine.

"This is the best time for satellites, isn't it Tom? We often come out after dinner to see how many we can spot. Our record's twelve."

"How can you tell they're satellites?"

"That's easy. They look like a star moving across the sky on a fixed course. The lower they are, the faster they travel."

"Like a shooting star?"

"No. Not that fast and they don't disappear. You can

track a satellite for quite a while."

We lay back in silence, waiting.

"There's number one." George pointed directly overhead as a bright dot floated across our patch of sky. Tom leapt up and raced along the garden path, as if to follow its course. He came back breathless, smiling.

"Who'll spot the next one?" I asked, shifting over, making room on the seat. "Here, come and sit with me."

Tom brushed against my feet as he sat and started to rub them.

"Yes. Cold aren't they?" I tucked them beneath me. "There, they'll be fine now."

He nodded, watched me for a moment, then went inside.

"Don't be long or you'll miss the next one," George teased. He turned to me, bottle in hand. "More wine?"

"No, thank you. I must go soon. Dinner was lovely. Perhaps you'll both risk a meal with me? I warn you though, I'm no match......."

Tom reappeared, his arms wrapped around something pale and feathery. Slippers. Delicate, backless slippers. He offered his gift.

"These were my mummy's."

George stifled a gasp.

And a swan danced with the moon.

"A penny for them, love." George sat down and smiled.

"Oh, they're worth much more than that." I returned his smile. "Ready for your breakfast?"

He patted his stomach. "I certainly am. Have you had yours?"

"Of course, hours ago."

"Don't give me that, this toast is still warm."

"Okay, Sherlock, here, have a menu."

"No need, thanks, I've already ordered." He glanced across the room. "And how are the boys this morning?"

"Gorgeous. High as kites. Too excited to be tired, despite the best stag night ever, if the rumours are correct."

"I'll bet they are."

"Here they come now, you can check for yourself."

They were lurching across the dining room, Edward dragging Tom in a brotherly headlock; Tom, taller by inches, feigning submission then lifting his brother clean off the ground.

They pulled up chairs on either side of their father, each draping an arm around his shoulders.

"How do Pop?"

"How do yourself, Ed? Learned to hold your liquor yet?"

"Not exactly hold, no. We were shifting it too fast for that."

George laughed. "And how about the groom?"

"Great, till I got a whiff of your bacon." Tom leant back, making room for the waiter. "Ah, coffee, I definitely need more coffee."

"And a headache pill, perhaps?" I offered him the pack.

"Cheers, Ma."

"Right, gentlemen." George laid down his knife and fork. "Are we ready?"

"We are."

"What? Ready for what?"

"You'll see, my lovely." He reached across and placed a small, leather box on the table in front of me. "This is from us. A token of our love and thanks. Designed by Tom, for a very special lady."

I looked at each in turn, vision blurring for the second time, then opened the box. It held a ring. A sparkling oval in a nest of deep blue stones.

"It's beautiful. Thank you." I lifted it from the box and slipped it on. "Perfect." I held out my hand, turning it from side to side.

"Look in the stone, Ma. There. Do you see it?"

"Yes. What is that?" Something white, feathery, had been caught in the quartz. "It's like....." I glanced up at Tom.

"Yes, I know." He was grinning now. "It looks like a swan."

Dryad –
One Story, Two Endings

The Beginning – Joanne Harris

In a quiet little corner of the Botanical Gardens, between a stand of old trees and a thick holly hedge, there is a small green metal bench. Almost invisible against the greenery, few people use it, for it catches no sun and offers only a partial view of the lawns. A plaque in the centre reads: In Memory of Josephine Morgan Clarke, 1912 – 1989. I should know – I put it there – and yet I hardly knew her, hardly noticed her, except for that one rainy Spring day when our paths crossed and we almost became friends.

I was twenty–five, pregnant and on the brink of divorce. Five years earlier, life had seemed an endless passage of open doors; now I could hear them clanging shut, one by one; marriage; job; dreams. My one pleasure was the Botanical Gardens; its mossy paths; its tangled walkways, its quiet avenues of oaks and lindens. It became my refuge, and when David was at work (which was almost all the time) I walked there, enjoying the scent of cut grass and the play of light through the tree branches. It was surprisingly quiet; I noticed few other visitors, and was glad of it. There was one exception, however; an elderly lady in a dark coat who always sat on the same bench under the trees, sketching. In rainy weather, she brought an umbrella: on sunny days, a hat. That was Josephine Clarke; and twenty–five years later, with one daughter married and the other still at school, I have never forgotten her, or the story she told me of her first and only love.

It had been a bad morning. David had left on a quarrel (again), drinking his coffee without a word before leaving for the office in the rain. I was tired and lumpish in my pregnancy clothes; the kitchen needed cleaning; there was nothing on TV and everything in the world seemed to have gone yellow around the edges, like the pages of a newspaper that has been read and re–read until there's nothing new left inside. By midday I'd had enough; the rain had stopped, and I set off for the Gardens; but I'd hardly gone in through the big wrought–iron gate when it began again – great billowing sheets of it – so that I ran for the shelter of the nearest tree, under which Mrs Clarke was already sitting.

We sat on the bench side–by–side, she calmly busy with her sketchbook, I watching the tiresome rain with the slight embarrassment that enforced proximity to a stranger often brings. I could not help but glance at the sketchbook – furtively, like reading someone else's newspaper on the Tube – and I saw that the page was covered with studies of trees. One tree, in fact, as I looked more closely; our tree – a beech – its young leaves shivering in the rain. She had drawn it in soft, chalky green pencil, and her hand was sure and delicate, managing to convey the texture of the bark as well as the strength of the tall, straight trunk and the movement of the leaves. She caught me looking, and I apologised.

"That's all right, dear." said Mrs Clarke. "You take a look, if you'd like to." And she handed me the book.

Politely, I took it. I didn't really want to; I wanted to be alone; I wanted the rain to stop; I didn't want a conversation with an old lady about her drawings. And yet they were wonderful drawings – even I could see that, and I'm no expert – graceful, textured, economical. She had devoted one page to leaves; one to bark; one to the tender cleft where branch meets trunk and the grain of the bark coarsens before smoothing out again as the limb performs its graceful arabesque into the leaf canopy. There were winter branches; summer foliage; shoots and roots and wind–shaken leaves. There must have been fifty pages of studies; all beautiful, and all, I saw, of the same tree.

I looked up the see her watching me. She had very bright eyes, bright and brown and curious; and there was a curious smile on her small, vivid face as she took back her sketchbook and said: "Piece of work, isn't he?"

It took me some moments to understand that she was referring to the tree. "I've always had a soft spot for beeches," continued Mrs Clarke, "ever since I was a little girl. Not all trees are so friendly; and some of them – the oaks and the cedars especially – can be quite antagonistic to human beings. It's not really their fault; after all, if you'd been persecuted for as long as they have, I imagine you'd be entitled to feel some racial hostility, wouldn't you?" And she smiled at me, poor old dear, and I looked nervously at the rain and wondered whether I should risk making a dash for the bus shelter. But she seemed quite harmless, so I smiled back and nodded, hoping that was enough.

"That's why I don't like this kind of thing," said Mrs Clarke, indicating the bench on which we were sitting. "This wooden bench under this living tree – all our history of chopping and burning. My husband was a carpenter. He never did understand about trees. To him, it was all about product – floorboards and furniture. They don't feel, he used to say. I mean, how could anyone live with stupidity like that?" She laughed and ran her fingertips tenderly along the edge of her sketchbook. "Of course I was young; in those days a girl left home; got married; had children; it was expected. If you didn't there was something wrong with you. And that's how I found myself up the duff at twenty–two, married – to Stan Clarke, of all people – and living in a two–up, two–down off the Station Road and wondering; is this it? Is this all?"

That was when I should have left. To hell with politeness; to hell with the rain. But she was telling my story as well as her own, and I could feel the echo down the lonely passages of my heart. I nodded without knowing it, and her bright eyes flicked to mine with sympathy and unexpected humour. "Well, we all find our little comforts where we can," she said, shrugging. "Stan didn't know it, and what you don't know doesn't hurt, right? But Stanley never had much of an imagination. Besides, you'd never have thought it to look at me. I kept house; I worked hard; I raised my boy – and nobody guessed about my fella next door, and the hours we spent together."

She looked at me again, and her vivid face broke into a smile of a thousand wrinkles. "Oh yes, I had my fella," she said. "And he was everything a man should be. Tall; silent; certain; strong. Sexy – and how! Sometimes when he was naked I could hardly bear to look at him, he was so beautiful. The only thing was – he wasn't a man at all."

Mrs Clarke sighed, and ran her hands once more across the pages of her sketchbook. "By rights," she went on, "he wasn't even a he. Trees have no gender – not in English, anyway – but they do have identity. Oaks are masculine, with their deep roots and resentful natures. Birches are flighty and feminine; so are hawthorns and cherry trees. But my fella was a beech, a copper beech; red–headed in autumn, veering to the most astonishing shades of purple–green in spring. His skin was pale and smooth; his limbs a dancer's; his body straight and slim and powerful. Dull weather made him sombre, but in the sunlight he shone like a Tiffany lampshade, all harlequin bronze and sun–dappled rose, and if you stood underneath his branches you could hear the ocean in his leaves. He stood at the bottom of our little bit of garden, so that he was the last thing I saw when I went to bed, and the first thing I saw when I got up in the morning; and on some days I swear the only reason I got up at all was the knowledge that he'd be there waiting for me, outlined and strutting against the peacock sky.

Year by year, I learned his ways. Trees live slowly, and long. A year of mine was only a day to him; and I taught myself to be patient, to converse over months rather than minutes, years rather than days. I'd always been good at drawing – although Stan always said it was a waste of time – and now I drew the beech (or The Beech, as he had become to me) again and again, winter to summer and back again, with a lover's devotion to detail. Gradually I became obsessed – with his form; his intoxicating beauty; the long and complex language of leaf and shoot. In summer he spoke to me with his branches; in winter I whispered my secrets to his sleeping roots.

You know, trees are the most restful and contemplative of living things. We ourselves were never meant to live at this frantic speed; scurrying about in endless pursuit of the next thing, and the next; running like laboratory rats down a series of mazes towards the inevitable; snapping up our bitter treats as we go. The trees are different. Among trees I find that my breathing slows; I am conscious of my heart beating; of the world around me moving in harmony; of oceans that I have never seen; never will see. The Beech was never anxious; never in a rage, never too busy to watch or listen. Others might be petty; deceitful; cruel, unfair – but not The Beech. The Beech was always there, always himself. And as the years passed and I began to depend more and more on the calm serenity his presence gave me, I became increasingly repelled by the sweaty pink lab rats with their nasty ways, and I was drawn, slowly and inevitably, to the trees.

Even so, it took me a long time to understand the intensity of those feelings. In those days it was hard enough to admit to loving a black man – or worse still, a woman – but this aberration of mine – there wasn't even anything about it in the Bible, which suggested to me that perhaps I was unique in my perversity, and that even Deuteronomy had overlooked the possibility of non–mammalian, inter–species romance.

And so for more than ten years I pretended to myself that it wasn't love. But as time passed my obsession grew; I spent most of my time outdoors, sketching; my boy Daniel took his first steps in the shadow of The Beech; and on warm summer nights I would creep outside, barefoot and in my nightdress, while upstairs Stan snored fit to wake the dead, and I would put my arms around the hard, living body of my beloved and hold him close beneath the cavorting stars.

It wasn't always easy, keeping it a secret. Stan wasn't what you'd call imaginative, but he was suspicious, and he must have sensed some kind of deception. He had never liked my drawing, and now he seemed almost resentful of my little hobby, as if he saw something in my studies of trees that made him uncomfortable. The years had not improved Stan. He had been a shy young man in the days of our courtship; not bright; and awkward in the manner of one who has always been happier working with his hands. Now he was sour – old before his time. It was only in his workshop that he really came to life. He was an excellent craftsman, and he was generous with his work, but my years alongside The Beech had given me a different perspective on carpentry, and I accepted Stan's offerings – fruitwood bowls, coffee–tables, little cabinets, all highly polished and beautifully–made – with concealed impatience and growing distaste.

And now, worse still, he was talking about moving house; of getting a nice little semi, he said, with garden, not just a big old tree and a patch of lawn. We could afford it; there'd be space for Dan to play; and though I shook my head and refused to discuss it, it was then that the first brochures began to appear around the house, silently, like spring crocuses, promising en–suite bathrooms and inglenook fireplaces and integral garages and gas fired central heating. I had to admit, it sounded quite nice. But to leave The Beech was unthinkable. I had become dependent on him. I knew him; and I had come to believe that he knew me, needed and cared for me in a way as yet unknown among his proud and ancient kind.

Perhaps it was my anxiety that gave me away. Perhaps I under–estimated Stan, who had always been so practical, and who always snored so loudly as I crept out into the garden. All I know is that one night when I returned, exhilarated by the dark and the stars and the wind in the branches, my hair wild and my feet scuffed with green moss, he was waiting.

"You've got a fella, haven't you?"

I made no attempt to deny it; in fact, it was almost a relief to admit it to myself. To those of our generation, divorce was a shameful thing; an admission of failure. There would be a court case; Stanley would fight; Daniel would be dragged into the mess and all our friends would take Stanley's side and speculate vainly on the identity of my mysterious lover. And yet I faced it; accepted it; and in my heart a bird was singing so hard that it was all I could do not to burst out laughing.

"You have, haven't you?" Stan's face looked like a rotten apple; his eyes shone through with pinhead intensity. "Who is it?"..............

First Ending – Joanne Harris

I spent the rest of the night under The Beech, wrapped in a blanket. It was windy, but not cold; and when I awoke the wind had dropped and I was lying under a glorious drift of purple–green foliage. When I returned to the house, I found that Stan had gone, taking his woodworking tools and a case of his clothes with him.

By the end of the week, Daniel had joined him; a boy of twelve needs his father, and besides, Dan had always been more Stanley's boy than my own. All the same, I was happy. I saw no–one, but I was not lonely. Instead I felt curiously free. With Stan and Daniel gone I sensed much more than I had previously and I spent much of my time under The Beech, listening to the sounds of movement in the earth and of grass popping and of slow roots growing, inch by inch, under the dark soil.

For the first time I was aware of everything; of birds high in the branches; of insects tunnelling under the bark; of water half a mile underground. I slept there every night. I forgot to eat. I even stopped drawing. Instead I lay for days and nights under the royal canopy of The Beech, and there were times when I was sure I could have grown roots of my own, sinking softly and sweetly into the ground, leaving no trace of myself. It was blissful. Time had no meaning; I forgot the language of haste and flesh. Twice, a neighbour called to me over the fence; but her voice was shrill and unpleasant, and I ignored her. It rained, but I didn't feel cold; instead I turned my face towards the rain and let it fall gently into my open mouth. It was all the sustenance I needed. As the days passed I understood that at last I was joining him, like the two lovers in the old myth – Baucis and Philemon, I think it was – who were turned into trees so that they would never be apart. I was supremely happy; I pulled the earth over me like a quilt and sank my fingers into the ground. It would be soon, I knew; already my limbs had taken root; even when I tried to move them,

I could not. The cries from over the fence were barely audible now; I turned my face into the soil like a sleepy child into a pillow; and all around me was the sound of The Beech; soothing; loving; calling.

But something was wrong; something disturbed us; we sensed it in our roots. A shrill voice, too high for us to hear; a movement, too fast for us to follow. The rats were back; the horrid pink rats; and as we slept and dreamed our cool, slow dreams, they rushed and scurried about us, squeaking and gnawing and harrying and pawing. I tried to protest, but I had lost my tongue. I was uprooted; their faces loomed above me and as we became I once again, I heard their voices – and that of The Beech, raised for the first time in sorrow and loss – drowning out the sound of the world below.

Oh my dear my sweet my

Call the ambulance she's

Oh my love

I awoke in a bed of clean white sheets to the realization that time had recommenced. Stan, I was told, had sat by my bed for fourteen nights; the nurses were filled with praise for his doglike devotion. It had been close, they said. I had been lucky. Pneumonia had set in; I was malnourished and dehydrated; a few more hours and they might have lost me. Stan, they said, had gone back to the house, but he returned soon enough, and though I tried not to hear him, I soon found that I had lost the knack.

"I'm sorry, love," he told me. "I should have recognised

the signs." Apparently it all fitted; the neurotic behaviour; the sexual disgust; the desire for solitude; the obsessive–compulsive studies of trees. A breakdown, that was all; and I would get better very soon, he promised, with good old Stan to look after me. That silly quarrel was all in the past; there never had been a fella; and very soon I'd be right as rain. And there was good news; he'd found a buyer for the house. First–time buyer; no chain; and before I knew it we'd be living in that little semi we'd always wanted, with a nice bit of garden and no bloody trees.

I struggled to speak and found that I could not. Stan took my hand and held it.

"Don't worry, love. It's all arranged. They're very nice people; they'll take good care of the house. Course, that big old tree'll have to go –"

My mouth worked.

"Course it will, love. It can't stay there; it blocks the light. Besides, I don't want to risk that sale. You go to sleep now, and don't you fret. I'm looking after you now."

I never did go back to the house. I don't think I could have borne it, knowing what I knew. I never saw the little semi, either; instead I moved out as soon as I could to a rented flat near the Botanical Gardens. Even so, Stan didn't give up. For almost a year he and Daniel called on me every Sunday. But there was nothing to say. They had saved my life, but I had left the best part of myself under The Beech, and there could be no going back to my old life, even if I had wanted to. Then one day, nearly twelve months after my release from hospital, he brought me a present wrapped in crepe paper. "Open it," he said. "I made it for you."

It was a wooden dish about two feet across. Roughly heart–shaped, it was made from a perfect cross–section of tree trunk, with concentric circles shimmering through the wood.

"Thought you'd like a reminder," said Stan. "Seeing as you were always so fond of it, and all."

Wordlessly, I touched the edge of the dish. It was smooth and cool and flawlessly polished. With the tip of my finger I found the place at the heart of the tree, and it might have been my imagination, but for a second I seemed to feel a shiver of response, as if I had touched some dying nerve. "It's beautiful," I said, and I meant it.

"Thanks, love," said Stan.

I keep the dish on my dining room table. She left it to me, you know, along with her sketch–books and her drawings of trees. She didn't have anyone else, poor old dear; Stan had been dead for ten years and she'd been living in a retirement home since then. The Willows, it was called. I tried to find Daniel, but there was no contact address. The lady at The Willows thinks he might be living in New Zealand, but no–one knows for sure.

In a quiet little corner of the Botanical Gardens,

between a stand of old trees and a thick holly hedge, there is a small green metal bench. Almost invisible against the greenery, few people use it, except for me. They're all too busy with their own concerns to stop and talk; besides, I don't need them any more. After all, I have the trees.

Second Ending – Pat White

I looked at him for a long time. I was heady with the thought that he would know the truth at last; I was ready to face the consequences whatever they might be.

Come with me. I told him. Stan's eyes made even darker by suspicion, drilled into me.

"Come where?"

You'll see, I told him and led the way back into the garden, sure he would follow. The wind was stronger now, flattening the folds of my nightdress against me. The first heavy drops of rain bounced around us and Stan shivered, pulling his dressing gown cord tighter but there was no going back; I could feel the laughter bubbling up. Reaching The Beech I turned and leant back against him, pressed my palms against his smooth bark and felt strength flow into me, giving me courage. Stan came towards us, his face in shadow, then stopped, feet planted squarely on the path.

"Where is he then, this fancy–man of yours?" he shouted over the noise."

She was watching me again, her brown eyes, even

brighter now searching mine as she reached for my hand. "I've kept this secret for so long, but I'm old now and it's time; I would love to tell it to you, my dear." For the third time that afternoon I found myself nodding.

"Here, I told him, you're looking at him. Then the storm broke and the garden was lit by lightning which showed Stan, eyes wide in confusion, searching for my lover. He took a step, then another, and with a yell darted behind The Beech. I felt his fists pounding the trunk, heard the rattle of leaves overhead.

"I'll not be made a fool of" he shouted, his words spattering my face. He grabbed my shoulder, his thumb pressing painfully into the hollow at my neck. "And there'll be no divorce, if that's what you're thinking."

His face became dark and ugly as he tried to drag me back to the house. The roar of thunder startled us both making Stan's grip loosen and we slipped on the wet grass. He was winded as he fell, recovered and began to crawl to where I lay sobbing and frightened. I looked up at The Beech, pleading for help, and saw a terrible shudder pass through him. His branches lifted and, with a wrenching groan, a great limb was torn from his side. It came crashing down on Stan; snapped his neck like a twig."

I gasped, my breath catching in my throat; my hands flew to cradle the swell of my unborn child. Concern showed in the lines of her face as she asked if I was all right then waited, gently rubbing the back of my hand.

"You look a little tired, dear. Perhaps we should get you home. Come along." Too stunned to refuse I let her lead me to the gate. On the bus we sat in silence and I didn't object when she rang the bell as we reached my stop; didn't hesitate to let her follow me into the house. In the kitchen I reached for the kettle but she took it from me. "I'll do it dear," she said, "you sit down."

With our tea poured we sat at the kitchen table and she continued. "Stan was dead, of course, I could see that at once so I telephoned an ambulance and waited. A freak accident, the doctor said when he arrived, and blamed it on the storm, but I knew differently. On that night Stan meant me harm and The Beech saved me with no thought for himself. It was the end of him, you see. I noticed his leaves begin to pale; gradually the handsome red–bronze lost its lustre. There was a dreadful wound where his limb was severed and a canker set in which nothing would cure. I knew then it was over; his spirit had gone.

Of course I didn't lose him, not completely." Her eyes recovered their sparkle. "That autumn I gathered husks with the fruit still tucked safely inside. I planted them where they would thrive," she smiled, "and be cared for. And I'll let you into another little secret, dear," she leafed through her sketchbook, "this magnificent specimen is one of his – I bequeath him to you," she rose to rinse our cups. "I know how you love them." Confused, I turned sharply towards her. "He's in the Arboretum if the fancy takes you. They call me Josephine, by the way, Josephine Clarke and I am so very glad we met." She bent to kiss my cheek. "And remember," she lifted my hand and ran her thumb across my ring, "sometimes when we've made a wrong choice – if we allow it – fate intervenes." As she pulled on her coat she looked out at the garden. "I'm glad to see that beech of yours doing so well; he had me worried for a while." Before I could gather myself enough to ask she had gone, leaving her sketchbook for me.

Suddenly everything seemed to spin; I gripped the table to calm myself, not daring to believe she'd spoken of things she couldn't have known. I went and stood beneath our beech, watched the setting sun dance upon his leaves, and remembered. We had made love here, David and I, beneath the canopy one late summer's eve. Urgently at first, his need matching my own, then more gently, with tenderness and the understanding that we had fallen out of love. The soft breeze was like silk sliding over my skin; the tree baked hot smelled of summer and red wine; the sun, filtered through bronze foliage, bathed us in an amber glow I will never forget. It marked the end of our marriage; and the bittersweet beginning of my daughter's life.

I went to the Botanical Gardens often, hoping to find Mrs Clarke. When I read of her death almost two years later, I was filled with a sadness that took me by surprise; and a resolve. I fetched the sketchbook, took Caitlin to her nursery, and drove to the Arboretum.

He didn't take long to find: standing proud, his purple–green spring foliage just as she'd described. He was taller than I'd imagined; ridges spiralling up his trunk added distinction and rose to a canopy bursting with life. In his shade was a bench of gently curved metal its colour toning, its lines in harmony with the branches above. I sank down onto it and wept.

The man sat beside me in silence and waited while my tears slowed. "Wisest tree in the woods, the beech, an old friend once told me. He'll always listen, she said, but you'll need to be patient if you want a reply. I made her this bench to ease the waiting. Ruary MacLaren, woodsman." he shook my hand.

We walk among the trees most evenings. He says the moonlight on my hair glints like dew on the hawthorn; in the dampening air he smells of pine forests on the breeze. But Sylvie, she sets the woods ablaze with her coppery curls – a gift from her father.

This ending was first entered into the BBC 'End of Story' competition.

Pied Attire

Cinderella hated shoes. Contrary to popular belief, she was not forced to go barefoot. It's true the footwear they gave her was practical – hobnail boots for gardening and hanging out the washing, schoolmarmy lace–ups for indoors – and very ugly. But she didn't care. No, what she craved was comfort. That and the need to feel the ground beneath her feet. She'd also like to be called by her given name, but that was probably too much to hope for.

"You have the most beautiful toes."

"I know, and I'd like to keep them that way." She stretched them wide, the better for him to appreciate them. It had become their habit, Ella and Geoffrey, to sit on a bench by the fire whenever he delivered the bread. Sometimes they'd even sneak a cup of tea.

"You coulda been a dancer, I reckon."

"Why do you say that?"

"Just look. The big toe and the next two, they're all in a line. Mark of a dancer, that is."

"And how would you know?" She prodded him playfully in the ribs.

"Went to dance classes, didn't I? I was pretty good. You should've seen me gavotte."

"Show me."

"Nah."

"Go on, please."

Geoffrey stood up, bowed and began to move gracefully around the floor. "I need a partner, come on, up you get."

Ella took his hand. "I don't know if I can."

"It's easy. Just follow me."

Within minutes she'd got the hang of it. They twirled and whirled, waltzed and minuetted.

"You're a natural, you are."

Flushed and delighted, Ella hugged him. "And you're a great teacher."

'Spose I could've been, but I had to give it up. Me Mum needed me to get a job after Gran came to live with us, though I still go and watch, sometimes.

"I won't get a chance either. Not while the snapper–slappers have a say. In fact, I think they're trying to cripple me."

"No. How?"

The front door slammed.

"Look out, they're back. Run!"

Ermintrude crashed through the kitchen door with so many parcels she almost stuck. Anastasia, equally keen and just as overloaded, ran into the back of her sister and bounced off. In the ensuing fight, boxes cascaded in every direction.

"Now look what you've done."

"Wasn't me."

"Was too. Ooh, I didn't see these." Ermintrude held up a yellow satin peep–toed shoe with an ankle–threateningly high heel. "Rossi, you know I love Rossi. I ought to have them."

"Well what about the diamante Ferragamos. I wanted the turquoise but you had to grab them."

"Did not."

"Did so."

The floor was a kaleidoscope of colour. Silks, satin, velvet, suede spilled across the tiles. Even the boxes were fabulous and, thought Ella, probably had a better chance of fitting. For Mean and Nasty, as Ella liked to call them, had enormous feet; big, gnarled, nobbled, ugly feet. And in their quest to find the perfect shoe, the one to conceal the defects, they bought hundreds of pairs, all extremely expensive, and all several sizes too small.

"See, I told you," yelled Ermintrude, "they look better on me." She hoist up her skirt, revealing a stubbly shin and a bulbous, blue–veined calf. She turned her tortured foot this way and that, admiring. Her instep had buckled with the effort and the cracked toenail peeping out exactly matched the yellow of the satin.

"Bet you can't walk in them."

"Can too."

"Prove it."

She levered herself off the chair, took a deep breath, and launched herself across the room, ankles wobbling and bottom stuck out.

"There. What did I tell you?" She was red–faced with effort as she grabbed the door frame, just in time.

Ella clamped a hand over her mouth. She knew what was coming.

"All they need is a little breaking in. You'll do that," she turned, almost snapping the heel, "won't you Smellerella?"

Just what Ella dreaded; now her feet would have to go where those had been, and goodness knows what they'd have left behind.

"Coo–eee. Bread and buns." Geoffrey stuck his head around the back door. "What are you doing?"

Ella was stuffing peeled potatoes into a blue suede Jimmy Choo. "Stretching these, the acid is supposed to soften the leather or something."

"Must be an easier way."

"I'm not putting them on, if that's what you're thinking."

"No, give us 'em here. I'll have a go. Won't hurt with these socks on, will they?" He began to strut around the kitchen in a passable imitation of Ermintrude. Soon they were both giggling so much he had to sit down.

Ella caught her breath. "Keep going, come on. There's another pair to do yet."

"What's the rush?"

"The dance contest. Next week."

"No. You're kiddin' me. Those two lumps? I'd have a better chance of winning meself......here, hang on, that's not such a bad idea." A grin spread across his face. "You and me. We could, you know. Bit of practice of a night, when they're all abed. What d'you say?"

"I'd say you'd lost your marbles. How could we? Even if I could get away, well," she spread her hands, "look at me. I'm a mess. It'd take....... a miracle."

"Tosh and tiddle. For one, how're they gonna know you ain't here if they ain't? And for two, me Gran knows a thing or two," he tapped the side of his nose, "about magic and stuff. I'll have a word. Now, make us a cuppa while I sort out them Moschinos."

The tap on the door was so soft, Ella didn't hear it. What she did hear was the argument.

"Useless! What kind of a way is that to make an entrance. Knock harder."

"I don't want to break it."

"What the door?"

"No, silly, the wand."

"Give it to me."

Deirdre was standing firm, arm purposefully raised, when the door opened. "Oh," she said.

"Oh," said Audrey.

"Yes?" said Ella, "May I help you?"

"No, dear, quite the opposite. We're here to help you. I'm Deirdre, Geoffrey's Gran. And this is my sister, Audrey."

They bustled their way into the kitchen.

"Mmm, cosy. I'll just settle myself here by the fire, dear, so I won't be in the way." Deirdre made herself at home.

"Mind if I take off my cloak? I like to get straight down to business."

Before Ella could answer, Audrey had shrugged it off and began patting and smoothing the acres of pink tulle which were threatening to get the better of her.

"I know, dear," she caught Ella's look, "it's not practical at all, but it is what people expect. I'd hardly be a credible godmother without the fairy frock now, would I?"

"You look a little confused, dear." Deirdre chipped in. "Weren't you expecting us?"

"Yes. No. That is, not two of you. And not, umm, a fairy. I thought you'd be a seamstress or something."

The two old biddies laughed, crinkling their faces. Deirdre gained control first.

"Seamstresses, what a hoot. Oh no, dear, we don't do things the hard way. At least, I used not to. But I forgot to renew my license, which is why I had to bring her." She pointed at her sister and lowered her voice. "We don't let her at it on her own, though, not since......"

"Right. I'm ready." The tulle had finally been placated. "Ella, come and stand here, where I can get a good look at you." Audrey began to walk slowly around her, tutting and prodding. "Not so bad. Not so bad at all. I'll have you fixed up in no time."

She started at the top, and worked her way down. There were one or two little hiccups. Ella's hair turned blue, briefly, but the godmothers sorted it out between them. And Ella was quite enjoying herself. Till they got to her feet.

"I see three inch heels, chisel toe, black velvet. Possibly slingback."

"No."

"What do you mean, 'no'? You must."

"I won't wear shoes. I hate them. They pinch, they hurt. They'll ruin my evening.......and my feet."

"Stuff and nonsense. We all wear shoes. It's the price we pay to be elegant, graceful, taller even. You cannot expect to be taken seriously if you're barefoot and that, dearie, is that." Audrey folded her arms across her sparkly bodice.

Ella glared, pondered, then let her gaze drop to the hem of Audrey's dress. "What shoes are you wearing?"

Audrey rearranged the tulle. "Appropriate ones."

"Let me see."

"No need, dear. I tell you, I am perfectly well shod."

"So show me. Or barefoot I stay."

Audrey turned to her sister for support.

"You'll have to show her Aud."

Slowly, and with great reluctance, Audrey gathered an armful of tulle.

"What are those?" Ella stared at two huge white padded things, seemingly enveloped in lace.

"Just a little invention of my own. Hi–tech high–tops, I call them. The lace is a touch of genius, don't you think?"

"And you want me tottering on three inch heels?"

"Now, don't take on so. You'll only have yours on for an hour, two at most. Whereas I'm on my feet all day long. I do a lot of godmothering. It's a tricky business, you know. Ah, Geoffrey, thank goodness. You tell her."

"Tell her what?"

All three women answered at once.

"There. What d'you think?"

Ella straightened her leg, turning her foot to the left and right. "Beautiful, absolutely beautiful."

"Good. Now hold still while I do the other one." Geoffrey dipped his brush in the purple paint and stroked a diagonal line from the base of her big toe to the outside of her ankle. He swapped to a finer brush and continued to paint a strap around her ankle and back across her instep to her little toe. With a paler lilac he completed the shoe's outline, then filled it in, taking care to leave no gaps.

"Hey, that tickles." Ella giggled as the brush dipped between her toes.

"I know. Right Gran, how're those roses coming along?"

"Nearly done, lad. I'd be quicker with my wand......"

"No chance."

"Ah well."

"Here we are, Geoffrey," Audrey came in from the garden, "will these do?" She held up what looked like a pair of kippers.

"Almost. Try and make 'em Ella's size, and silver."

Finally, Geoffrey was satisfied. Ella's delicately painted feet rested on silver soles with pretty kitten heels. They were held in place by the finest gossamer, criss–crossed around her instep and ankle. A silver rose adorned each middle toe. The effect was magical.

"Go on then, try 'em out."

Tentatively at first, Ella stepped across the kitchen, then twirled into the perfect pirouette. "Geoffrey, you're a genius. They're wonderful."

"Thank godmothers for that. Right, let's be off. We've got a competition to win."

And win they did. The audience was spellbound. The judges were enchanted. Ella, they said, seemed to float on a cloud, following her partner's every move. Geoffrey, they said, was masterful. The pair were made for one another.

They left as the clock stuck midnight, skipping down the road, delighted by the evening and engrossed in their plans for the next.

"Ouch, what was that?" Geoffrey bent to pick up the offending object. "A shoe, glass by the looks of it." He handed it to Ella.

"You wouldn't catch me wearing that," she said, and tossed it over her shoulder as they continued on their way.

Affairs of the Heart

Dinner

The invitation was a surprise. I hadn't known Charles was back in England and was pleased but anxious at the thought of seeing him again. As I pushed my way through the heavy oak doors, designed to prevent as much as to permit my entrance, I spotted him at once. He sat in the far corner of the room, his head turned to the left, engaged in animated conversation with someone hidden from my view by the green leather wing of an armchair.

I paused to look at my watch. I wasn't early, but perhaps with that peculiar convention we Brits observe I ought to have been late. To interrupt or not I wondered? Something in the way Charles leant towards his companion suggested not. I turned, about to slip into the bar when he called my name.

"Michael, my friend. Come."

As I wove my way amongst the high–backed leather chairs, grouped intimately in the softly–lit room, I saw Charles reach forward to touch the other's arm and offer, I presumed, a few words of introduction.

"Charles, good to see you." I extended my hand.

He stood and clasped it warmly, clapping me on the shoulder with his free hand in that familiar way of his before waving it expansively in the direction of the other chair.

"Let me introduce you to Pieter, Pieter Strindberg. Pieter, meet Michael."

We shook hands as strangers are wont to do – briefly, with a firm grasp and a hint of appraisal in the eyes.

"Pieter and I met in Helsinki some years ago when I visited the Embassy. He was a visitor too and we were thrown together somewhat." They exchanged smiles. No corresponding explanation of me seemed to be required. "In fact, and I hope you won't think it too much of an imposition, Michael, I have asked Pieter to dine with us."

"Of course," I nodded, feeling more than a little imposed upon. I had wanted Charles to myself this evening, having not seen him for the last four months. And something else bothered me – something about Pieter which I could not quite identify.

We made polite and cheerful small talk over whiskey and soda until our waiter produced the menus. I made my selection quickly, gratified to see the old favourites still listed, and gave myself time to study the younger man. Early thirties, I estimated. His hair was light brown, blond in places from time spent in the sun if the colour of his skin was any indication. Cut unfashionably long, it curled where it touched his collar.

He was impeccably dressed. The cream linen of his shirt accentuated his tan and complimented the midnight blue suit. I shifted my gaze to his throat, noticed the gap between neck and collar and the knot of his cream and blue tie puffed out like a robin's breast in appropriate tribute.

He was strongly built. Even as he sat, I could sense powerfully muscled shoulders contained by the fabric of his jacket. His hands, splayed against the dark leather of the menu, were a contradiction; wide of palm with long, thick fingers which ended in perfectly, if severely, manicured nails. But the skin was too pale, too soft, in contrast to the strength they so clearly possessed.

He looked up suddenly, aware perhaps that he was being watched. Our eyes met for an instant. I turned my attention to the wine list with that uncomfortable feeling of having been caught out.

Our waiter reappeared to lead us into the dining room and, once seated, conversation resumed. Pieter entertained us with stories of Helsinki and the Embassy but was rather vague about the purpose of his visit, even when pressed.

"Oh, just one of the guests invited to celebrate the opening of the new Embassy. You know how it is, I'm sure." He looked directly at me. "Making up the numbers probably, since I happened to be in Helsinki."

"Are you often there?"

"Yes, quite often. I take care of one or two things for

our diplomatic colleagues across most of Scandinavia." His tone implied no more would be revealed. "The Embassy caused something of a stir actually. Have you seen it yourself?"

I shook my head.

"You really should. It's a curvaceous masterpiece of steel and smoky glass, strangely at odds with the Ambassador's Residence. I believe most of the opposition came from the putative potentates in the Embassies nearby. The Finns, with their ability to embrace both the high–tech and the traditional, are rather more pragmatic in my experience."

Charles, unusually quiet throughout, looked on with a paternal, or proprietorial, smile and the occasional nod. This served only to add to my discomfiture. I began to worry that we might not have the opportunity to speak alone, yet he must surely be curious.

When my turn came to carry the conversation I struggled to lighten my mood. I began to fill in the gaps of the last months, mostly for Charles, of course, since it would hold very little relevance for Pieter, I imagined.

"I've been abroad myself, perhaps Charles mentioned?"

Pieter shook his head. "Doing what exactly?" His directness took me by surprise, as did his interest.

"One of a team observing the withdrawal of the US Navy from a particularly beautiful Caribbean island. Negotiations became rather tricky, you know how it is."

Pieter raised an eyebrow. "No, I can't say that I do."

Ruffled, I continued. "Problems of rights and access to land and property, that sort of thing. Our presence was supposed to instil calm and diffuse hostility."

"And did you?"

"Humph! Hardly. Not yet anyway. Too many voices and vested interests. But I suppose 'justice' of sorts has been seen to be done. We're due back in a week or so for the next stage of the process."

Charles looked up. "Do you know when exactly?"

"I don't, not yet." A look I couldn't identify passed across his face. "Why, is there anything.....?"

"No, no. I just wondered." He lifted his napkin, wiped his fingers carefully then replaced it on the table. "Will you excuse me? I won't be a moment."

As I watched him leave the room my concern increased. He seemed weakened somehow, less in control. Not the Charles I had expected to find this evening.

Left to ourselves we had little to say to one another. Pieter toyed with the remains of his dinner while I signalled to the waiter for more wine.

"He's been an awfully long time don't you think? I'd better just...."

"Stay there, I'll go." Pieter was out of his chair and gone before I could comment. I lifted my glass and drained it in one.

By the time Pieter returned I had made up my mind. There were things I had to know.

"Charles is fine," he assured me, "he'll be back directly."

"Look here, I......"

"We're not lovers, he and I, in case you were wondering?" He tilted his head. "My business with Charles is an entirely different affair and, as a matter of fact, none of yours. Unless, that is, Charles sees fit to........." he glanced across the room. "Ah, here he comes now."

Michael

I have no recollection of leaving the club, much less hailing a taxi but I supposed that John, the night porter, must have seen to that for me. I asked the driver to stop as we neared Regent's Park – that I do remember – and climbed out. Too much wine, and my concern for Charles, had left me feeling decidedly edgy. I hoped a walk would dispel my unease or at least allow me to review the events of the evening.

When Charles returned to our table he had seemed unwell. There was a sheen of perspiration across his forehead which he kept dabbing, ineffectually, with his handkerchief. I tried to draw him aside.

"Charles, I wonder if we might have a word?"

He had looked across at me.

"In private."

He appeared to consider my request. "I'm sorry, Michael, but I'm suddenly rather tired. You'll have to excuse me." He stood. "But I'll be in touch. Soon." And with that, he left.

I sat back, watching in disbelief as he went. Having the distinct impression that Pieter would intervene should I attempt to follow, I had remained seated while he settled the bill, said a terse goodnight, and walked away.

I felt little better for the exercise. Standing on the steps at my door I had no idea how long I'd walked or the route I'd taken. As I ransacked my pockets in search of the key, I was overcome with the kind of weariness which demands sleep, but will not allow it.

The house felt hot. I went upstairs to my study and opened the french doors onto the small balcony which overlooked the square. Apart from one or two lights in the windows opposite and the occasional car, there was little sign of life. Usually I found the view and the quiet soothing, but not tonight.

I collected a tumbler from the kitchen and poured a generous measure of Scotch knowing it would add to my wakefulness, but I needed to think; to try and make sense of the evening, and Charles.

He was not my first lover although there had not been many, the need for discretion being so much a part of my way of life. He loved me, of that I had always been certain. We had gone beyond that insistent, lustful, rapaciousness of the early days to something more tender and much more precious. Why now did I have occasion to doubt? That touch of the hand. I was unable to drive it from my mind.

We'd met at a conference in Lisbon five years ago. Charles was with a delegation from the British Council; I worked for the Gulbenkian Foundation and, among other things, had organised the site-seeing trips which formed an obligatory component of such gatherings. By the third afternoon I was escorting a party of only two, Charles and a rather earnest young woman for whom Gulbenkian, the oil tycoon and philanthropist, was something of a hero. She had, I recalled with gratitude, declined Charles' request that we dine with him.

We had drinks in the bar at his hotel. He had impressed me at once with his candour; the willingness with which he told me about himself and his life. In return, I had revealed aspects of myself I would not normally have told.

Our dinner was splendid. The reputation for excellence of the newly refurbished Avenida Palace Hotel was well deserved. As the wine relaxed us our conversation grew more intimate. When he asked if we could meet on his next trip to Lisbon, reaching across to place the briefest touch on the back of my hand, I had the feeling we might be meeting for a long time to come.

I awoke with a start. The empty glass was lying on the carpet next to the chair in which I had finally fallen asleep. My neck hurt, my clothes were crumpled and I had a raging thirst. After several glasses of water and a hot shower, I was ready to face myself in the mirror. As I wiped away the steam and stared at my reflection, I was surprised not to find the anguish of the previous night etched more deeply. There were dark, bluish shadows beneath my eyes, but nothing else to reveal how I felt.

I ran my palm down each cheek, the back of my fingers from throat to chin, taking comfort from the ritual. With slow, circular movements I raised a lather which smothered my stubble, contorted my face to tighten the skin then drew the blade from cheekbone to jaw. That first sweep of the razor wiped away my indecision. I needed to speak to Charles.

With my face still smarting from the cologne, I dialled and waited, a small knot of tension lodged just under my ribs. The familiar voice confirmed what I had feared; he was not at home. I telephoned the club on the off chance there would be a message. There was not, but an efficient factotum informed me that Charles had left early this morning. For Helsinki.

This time I did not hesitate. Several telephone calls later I had secured a seat on an evening flight next day. Clutching my briefcase I left for the office, preparing my apologies along the way.

Charles

I was cleared through diplomatic channels at Helsinki's Vantaa airport in record time. The Ambassador had sent a man to meet me, for which I was grateful. Settled into the back of the limousine, I paid little attention to our route, except to notice that he chose Mannerheim Street which took us past the stunning white–tiled Opera House, the National Museum and Parliament Buildings. He must have thought me a newcomer to the city.

As we drove through the wrought–iron gates into the gravelled courtyard, Pieter's words sprang to mind; the Residence and Embassy buildings did indeed make incongruous neighbours.

"Welcome, Mr Sidwell." Smiling, Eeva held back the door. "It is a pleasure to have you with us again."

"Thank you, Eeva. It's good to be back." The strain in my voice must have been obvious.

"We've put you in your usual room sir. May I take your valise?"

"No, thank you Eeva. I'll take it up myself ."

It was a relief to be alone. I was glad the Ambassador was away, though somewhat ashamed to be so. Normally I would have enjoyed an evening en famille, but I knew I should have been dull company that evening. Once in my room I could hold thoughts of Michael at bay no longer. His expression, usually so inscrutable, had revealed disappointment and confusion. He had made his decision, that was clear, and wanted to tell me. The irony of it. I had waited so long but did not want his answer now, not yet.

When I came down to breakfast there was a message from Pieter. He was unable to meet me as arranged

– something urgent – but one of his colleagues would collect me at reception. This served only to add to my anxiety. I had wanted the comfort of a familiar face.

Just before midday my taxi delivered me to the front of an anonymous red brick building, tucked down a side street but still within sight of the sea. I took a few moments to compose myself then pushed through the heavy wooden doors with a show of bravado I did not feel.

I was unused to hospitals. The low–level lighting and plush furnishings offered little comfort to one so nervous. Scent from a huge vase of lilies on the desk did not quite disguise the antiseptic undertones. I announced myself to the receptionist and was asked to wait while she let them know I had arrived. My feeble attempt at distraction, leafing through the magazines provided, was hopeless. I gave up after a while and resigned myself to the wait.

"Mr Sidwell?"

"Yes." I stood and took the proffered hand.

"I'm Alex. Come this way."

I followed her though heavy glass doors, down several flights of stairs and into a warren of brightly lit corridors. We turned left into what appeared to be a locker room where I was given a set of clothes, like green pyjamas, and told to change.

"Knock on that door," Alex pointed, "once you are ready and I'll help with the cap and mask."

It seemed to take an age. I fumbled with laces, pulled off my shoes then wondered if I should have. I folded my suit, stacked it as neatly as I could on one of the benches and pulled on the trousers and tunic. The knot in my stomach tightened as I padded across the floor and tapped as instructed. The smell of antiseptic as the door opened was overwhelming. I grasped the door frame as the room began to spin.

"Are you sure you want to do this?" Alex was brusque.

"Of course. Yes." I took a deep breath. "I'm just rather hot."

She studied my face for a moment but accepted the explanation. "Turn around." She tied the cap securely at the back of my head. "Pinch this across the bridge of your nose," she handed a gauzy mask over my shoulder then knotted those tapes too. The white slip–ons she dropped at my feet were spattered yellow and brownish red.

"Do they fit?"

I nodded.

"Come."

The narrow passage led to a single door.

"This is a sterile area." She began to scrub her hands and forearms at a steel sink. "When we go into theatre I'll show you exactly where to stand. You must not touch anything. Nothing at all, is that clear?"

I nodded and she shouldered her way through the door.

I had never before been in an operating theatre and was ill–prepared for it. The room was smaller than I had imagined and extremely bright. The operating table occupied its centre; several people, all but one unidentifiable behind masks and caps, were occupied with cylinders, monitors and various other instruments. An immense circular light shone down onto the body of a man. He was draped in green. Tubes and wires issued from under the sheets. His chest, which had been shaved, was being painted with yellow liquid.

I was positioned at his head, relieved that my view of his face was obscured, with the anaesthetist slightly in front and to my left. She and Alex exchanged a few words before Alex called for a tray, watched while the sealed wrapper was torn off and dried her hands on the paper towel inside. She pulled on sterile gloves and took her place beside the surgeon, Pieter. He acknowledged me with a nod.

"Ready?" Pieter surveyed his colleagues. "Then let's begin."

The long incision down the centre line of the man's chest was oddly bloodless; the smell of charred flesh was intense. The anaesthetist had shifted towards me.

"Is he still on his feet?" Pieter had not looked up.

"He is." She shifted back.

"Excellent. That's the first hurdle over. Stryker." Alex passed him the saw.

The gleaming blade whirred into life. As it bit into

80

bone my knees turned to liquid and would no longer support me.

"Get him out. Now."

I came to in the scrub room. Someone had propped me up on a bench across from the sinks. I felt weak and nauseous, mortified by my collapse and the trouble it had caused. I could hear voices raised in a heated argument and, as Pieter burst through the door......

".....strictly no observers. A step too far even for us, wouldn't you say?"

"I would not," boomed Pieter, "and I'll tread where I will." He tore off his gloves, hurled them into a bin behind the door and began furiously scrubbing his hands.

"I apologise, Pieter. I don't know...."

"It happens. Are you well enough to leave?"

It was clear that my returning to the operating theatre was not a consideration. I nodded.

"Good. I'll arrange it. Take a walk, get some air, relax if you can. We'll meet at the restaurant this evening. 6.30."

When my escort arrived, Pieter was still attacking his hands.

I felt better outside, glad to have left the reminders of mortality behind. I found my way to the shore and turned towards the harbour, walking along the gritted paths that hug the water's edge. The sea never failed to calm me, conjuring up memories of long hot summers on Cornish beaches, home for the holidays and endless adventure. Even today it worked its magic. By the time I had reached the first of the small cafes dotted along my route, I felt well enough to go inside and risk a cup of something. Although long past lunchtime, I could not yet face the prospect of food.

Some 30 minutes later, revived and feeling much more my old self, I headed back to the Embassy to shower and change before dinner.

The number 4 tram leaves from the heart of the city on a circular route to Munkkiniemi, the Monk's nose, a suburb to the west of the city built along the curve of a sea inlet. It is a beautiful area. Old villas, used in times past as summer houses by the rich and by royalty, have been well maintained and now house museums or restaurants and cafes. I reached the restaurant Solna in plenty of time, ordered myself a glass of wine and sat at one of the outside tables to enjoy the evening sun.

Pieter arrived exactly at 6.30. The day's exertions did not seem to have left their mark. We moved inside, ordered more wine and studied the menu.

"The food is excellent here." He gave full attention to his selection. I did the same.

Our waiter, a small man whose white wraparound apron reached almost to the floor, stood discreetly nearby. Knowing precisely the right moment, he moved forward swiftly, pen in hand, then headed purposefully for the kitchen.

I took a gulp of wine, fortifying myself. "Pieter, this afternoon....."

He held up his hand, but I pressed on regardless.

"I need to explain."

"Unnecessary."

"Listen. Please. I am not of a nervous disposition, nor am I unusually squeamish. But I didn't expect it to be so brutal."

Pieter took a long drink from his glass and looked at me steadily. "Do you imagine I'll be less brutal with you?"

Disclosure

I was led through an elegant reception hall into a smaller withdrawing room. I remember the smell of the roses – almost too powerful – tumbling from a huge bowl onto the polished table.

"Mr Winsford is here, sir."

Charles stood, seemingly lost in thought, at an arched window overlooking the garden. "There's a romantic tale associated with this place, you know. Years ago, long before the Embassy was built, there was an uninterrupted view of the fortress on the island of Suomenlinna. A beautiful princess, whose family owned the house, fell in love with a sea captain billeted there. At night, whenever it was safe, she would light a candle in this window as a signal, and wait for her lover to row across."

"I came without the candle, Charles."

"Yes, you did," as he turned, a smile stole across his face, "I'm delighted to say. Come, sit and let's have coffee. It's time I explained, don't you think?" He sipped his coffee. "Michael, I am ill."

I drew a breath to speak.

"No, let me go on. It seems my coronary arteries are blocked, three of them. I need surgery, major surgery, but the outlook is good, apparently."

"How long have you known?"

"Not long."

"And you didn't think to tell me?"

"I couldn't. I was afraid it would sway your decision; make you say yes for the wrong reasons."

"How could there be wrong reasons, Charles?" I was angry, disappointed that he thought me so shallow, and deeply concerned for his health. I fought for control of my voice. "How did you find out?"

"At a routine medical. Well not exactly routine, slightly more thorough than usual. You see, a rather high level post has come up in Brussels, and I was asked if I were interested."

"And when was I to hear about that?"

"It was to be a surprise, Michael. I know how you love Brussels. And, if I'm honest, I hoped you would see it as a great opportunity; an opportunity for us to be together."

"That's as may be." I bit on my anger, turned it to sarcasm. "Was I to have a say in the matter?"

"Of course. I'm so sorry." he rubbed his hands across his face, his distress plain. "I seem to have got everything wrong. I never intended to put you through this. "

"You'll forgive me for thinking that you had changed your mind. In London, that business with Pieter."

"Ah yes, that dreadful evening. I had planned to tell you about Brussels, sure you would be delighted. I didn't believe I was ill, I had no symptoms. But the test results confirmed it. It was Pieter who brought them."

"How so?"

"He's a surgeon, Michael, a cardiac surgeon. He will do the operation."

"Why him? Is he capable? Do you know that he is?"

"He's the surgeon of choice in diplomatic circles, where discretion is as valued as skill. And yes, he is more than capable; he is known as the best."

I struggled to take this in. "When?"

"The day after tomorrow."

"Why so soon?" The possibility of losing him struck like a blow.

"No, no," he placed a hand on my arm, "the urgency is Pieter's not mine. He has a busy schedule it seems. Still, the sooner the better. Literally, let's hope." He gave a wry laugh.

"'Outcome', 'schedule', how can you be so flippant? I clenched my fists to conceal the shaking. "Aren't you afraid at all?"

"A little, yes, but resigned to my fate. Probably the result of seeing him in action."

"What?"

"Another mistake as it turns out, but the intentions were good. Forewarned and all that..... Michael", his voice softened as he looked at me, "I've been a fool, I know I have, but I really am so glad you're here. Will you come to the hospital with me?"

"Of course. Where else would I be?"

The Ambassador had invited me to stay but I decided not. I was in no mood for company or conversation. I had booked into an hotel in the city centre and retreated there.

The next day I was of little use to Charles, I'm ashamed to say, recent events having left me shaken. I accompanied him to the hospital, sat in a side–room while he underwent more tests and answered questions. Finally, a nurse came to fetch me and took me to join him.

"Not bad, is it?" Charles was settled on a small sofa wearing pyjamas and dressing gown. The bed was discreetly screened from view. "I'd have preferred to keep my suit on but the rules......." He gave a shrug. "Perhaps they think I'll run."

He seemed at ease, unworried. I felt helpless.

"There's no need for you to spend the whole day here, you know. I'll be fine. Go and explore."

I did as he asked, sensing it was for the best, but could find little outside the hospital to hold my attention.

The city wakened early, as did I. In truth, I had hardly slept. I left the hotel before six, needing to be on the move. I turned away from the railway station and its bustle of activity, walked through the cobbled square and onto a wide tree–lined street. A garden running the whole of its length offered solitude and a place to sit. For most of the night I had wrestled for control of my panic. The disquiet I had felt in London was as nothing compared to this. And the knowledge that Pieter was a skilled surgeon did not temper my dislike of the man. But that was irrelevant now. Charles had faith in him; so must I.

He was sitting up in bed when I arrived looking strangely young and vulnerable in the pale hospital gown. He reached for me as I sat at his side but his movement was restricted by the tube attached to the back of his hand.

"You'll excuse me for not getting up, this thing" he plucked at the gown, "has no back to it." The smile did not fool me, but his attempt at humour was touching.

"Did you sleep at all?"

"Well enough. And you?"

"Not really. Charles, I........ A nurse appeared, armed with a syringe.

"Just something to help you relax, Mr Sidwell."

We both looked away as she dealt with the injection, then sat, waiting, in that rigid silence that keeps terror at bay.

Some time later the porters arrived, checked the name tag fastened to his wrist, and lifted him onto a trolley.

"Come with me Michael."

"Of course." I glanced at one of the porters.

"As far as theatres, sir. Then we take him."

We wove our way through narrow corridors brightly lit by fluorescent tubes. Oddly, I wondered if they hurt his eyes, lying as he was, staring up at them.

"This is where we leave you, sir."

We had stopped in front of a pair of frosted glass doors. One of the porters pressed a button on the wall.

"Michael, I need to ask, what would have been your answer?" There was an urgency to his question and he struggled to sit up.

"It would have been, and remains, yes."

"Thank you." He slumped back.

The doors slid apart to reveal Pieter, gowned ready for surgery but with his mask drawn down. He held my gaze, steadily, for several moments then, unaccountably, his eyes softened. He gave the briefest nod, then turned, and followed Charles.

Choose Any Suitor

I'm not a dreamer. That is to say I must have dreams, we all do, but I can never remember them. Sometimes I almost do, in those gauzy moments between sleep and waking, but they hover just beyond my grasp, tantalising, and slip further away the more I reach. Until now, that is.

'Any suit for a tenner', the sign said, – a bargain by any standards – so I went in. I don't usually fancy second hand clothes. No matter that they're nearly new or have just been cleaned, there's a certain mustiness about them which puts me off. Still, with that end of term party coming up, I thought I'd have a browse, look for inspiration.

There was the usual rack of shirts just inside the door; an odd assortment of coats all along one wall; skirts and trousers jostling for space. All were pale and tired–looking. Nothing to interest me.

"Is there anything else?" I asked the man behind the counter.

"Try through there," he said, pointing to an archway behind him. "I'm sure you'll find what you want."

I stepped into a riot of colour. Taffeta, satin, net and lace seeming to dance around me. Racks of shoes to match or fashioned in gold and silver. Dinner jackets in dark jewel colours, stylish partners for any ball gown. An array of wraps, and a feather boa or two, drifting into rainbows across the walls. I gazed around and there it was, draped casually over a dressmaker's dummy. A black tuxedo. Perfect.

I lifted it off, slipped the sleeves over my arms, feeling the red, silk lining slide over my fingers. I ran my hands down the cool, satin lapels, smooth except for a small snag in the cloth. I fastened the single button, brushed at a powdery patch on one shoulder. I could get that off later. When I turned to the mirror I was startled by my transformation, from student to siren. My legs seemed longer, cleavage highlighted in the deep satin V. I piled my hair on top of my head, turned this way and that, pleased with the effect. A pair of fishnet tights and some perilously high heels would complete the outfit.

It was still a tenner, he told me, even without the trousers. Or I could hire something else, get half my money back next day. But I said not. I knew the tuxedo had to be mine.

It was crumpled by the time I got home that night, and I'm no good with the iron. So I turned the shower to hot, let it run till the bathroom was really steamy, and hung it from the rail while I stood under the spray.

As the steamy tendrils enfolded us, the fabric smoothed and freshened, seemed to relax into a whole new shape.

Back in the bedroom I hooked the hanger over the wardrobe door, not wanting to squeeze it in amongst the clutter. The powder had almost gone, the snag on the lapel hardly showed at all. I drifted into sleep and as I did, I imagined the tuxedo coming to life.

The dress I wear is red, bias cut to hug my hips and then swirl to the ground. The straps are thin, sequinned, and the plunge at the back reaches way down to the dimples at the base of my spine. That's where his hand rests. The music begins, and he holds me close, draws me into his body, thigh between thighs. He is tall and strong and steers me through the tango. Each stamp of his foot draws shouts from the crowd. Each kick of my heel paints an arc of red silk, and the flick of our heads adds passion and drama. With cheek pressed to cheek we stride across the floor then, as the dance ends, I fall back in his arms and he bends to place a kiss on my throat. To thunderous applause we leave the salon, go out onto the deck to the inky darkness. He slips his arm around me, I rest my face against his shoulder, content.

This one tugs playfully at the knot of my sarong. We're walking along hibiscus–lined paths on our way to the Great Room, and dinner. It will be a splendid affair to celebrate its opening. The hotel is fabulous, in the style of the old plantation houses, when sugar cane was a major crop. We hear music through the open shutters, reminding us of the island's past. The breeze is warm, caressing; the tree frogs are calling their two–note song, and the scent of gardenias is intoxicating.

The oaken doors are opened as we approach, by staff dressed in glorious colours for the occasion. The room is magical, flowers and candles on every table and tiny white lights strung high up among the beams. We are led to ours by a beautiful young woman. She pours champagne into tall flutes and offers the menu. We drink to one another, glasses clinking, eyes locked. He lifts my hand and plants a kiss on my wrist. I pull a pin from my hair, pluck a red hibiscus from the vase and fasten the bloom to his lapel.

The London night is chill, after the warmth of the theatre. We stroll along the Jubilee Walk humming songs from the show. We giggle as we remember the star, bare–bottomed, swoop Tarzan–like across the stage. We're wondering which train to catch but we're in no hurry, want to make the evening last. We know a place just perfect for a night–cap.

The lights reflected in the water twinkle with the breeze; we watch the progress of an old barge heading up river, the dark tail of its wake just visible as it passes. We hear the growl and thwack of skateboard wheels on concrete, athletic young men performing for fun. The Millennium bridge extends an invitation to jump up and down and make it wobble. I shiver and he slips his jacket around my shoulders, pulls up the lapels, fastens the single button. Behind him I see the London Eye wink.

I awake exhausted, the bed a tangle. I lie still, remembering, amazed. The colours, the sounds, I can smell the gardenias. I drift through the day, revisiting my dreams. When evening comes I reach for the tuxedo, take it off its hanger. I slip my arms into the sleeves to feel the cool touch of silk. I brush the shoulder lightly, run my hands down the lapels, fasten the single button, slide my hands into the pockets. My fingers touch something, an envelope. I open it, unfold the note which bears three names, three telephone numbers.

Inspired by Thomas Hardy's poem – A Gentleman's Second–hand Suit.

Many a Slip........

The letter didn't arrive till the following week, so you can imagine how upset I was.

'Dear Mrs Morrison,' it said.

'As you may know resources in the NHS, your NHS, are overstretched. While we do our very best with our allocation, we have to make economies. But let me assure you that patient care is our priority. **'Your needs, Our musts'.** *The Trust's new slogan, of which we are justly proud.*

You will also be aware of demographic changes. There are far more elderly people who, by definition, will place heavier demands on our services than resources allow. As a result, and after a lengthy period of consultation, we have formulated a plan, the success of which depends on your cooperation.'

Does it indeed? Well how was I supposed to cooperate, when I didn't even know there was a plan?

It was a Tuesday, I remember it well. I generally go to the Post Office in St Aldates on a Monday, but our Sandra popped in, so I left it a day. I never take the bus. It's only half a mile or so and the walk does me good. I come along Paradise Street, up Castle Street, past the

Westgate Centre and into Marks – it's a bit off the track but I do like their displays – then out the back door into Pembroke Street. I'd just stepped off the kerb and wham. Upended I was, by a cyclist of all things. I was glad of me trousers, I can tell you, or I would've been the one on display.

Very nice about it, he was. Said it wasn't my fault, he'd seen me clear as day. I thought that was funny, to tell the truth, and wondered why he hadn't braked, or swerved at least. Next thing, he's off his bike, whips this piece of paper out of his rucksack and starts asking me questions. He sounded that official, and with me being in shock, probably, I answered them.

'How do you feel?' Well, that was daft. How did he think I'd feel? Shaken, I told him, definitely shaken.

'Can you stand?' he asks.

'I am, aren't I? Look'.

'Ah yes,' he says, 'but is your weight evenly distributed?'

I begged his pardon at that one. 'What?'

'Can you stand on both feet together, and one at a time?'

Well, I did feel a ninny hopping from foot to foot in the middle of Pembroke Street, but I passed that test. He went on some more about wrists and shoulders, blurred vision, waggled a finger in front of my eyes, then.....

'Very Good, Mrs Morrison,' he says. 'You've done really well.'

'But...'

'Very well indeed.'

Then hands me this letter, addressed and all. 'Take this to your GP soon as you can. He's expecting it. Thank you so much for your co–operation. Goodbye.'

I took a moment to gather myself, went to the Post Office, then straight home. I was tempted, as you can imagine, to open the envelope. But you don't do you? Not when there's doctors involved. I meant to take it round the next day then the phone rang – it was our Sandra – and I completely forgot.

The following Monday it all comes back to me. 'Ooo Dolly, the envelope', I says to myself. Before I can get it from behind the clock the postman comes. And brings the letter I was telling you about.

'The demand for diagnostics in our area,' it goes on, 'bone densitometry for example, has reached epic proportions.'

I'm not quite sure what this bone thing is, but I read on anyway, hoping I'll find out.

'Unfortunately it is very expensive, but we know its importance to ladies of a certain age. In consultation with our experts, therefore, we have devised a new screening method. It is low cost, totally safe, and being trialled in your area. We know you will want to participate.'

But I might not, did he think about that? Blooming cheek, making assumptions. And once I saw that plan of his I certainly wouldn't.

'Sometime during the next week, you'll be involved in a little incident. No need for concern since you will be totally safe and one of our Doctors–in–Training, not a

junior doctor – *some of them are rather mature* – *will be in attendance throughout. I am unable to give further detail at this point, suffice to say that the element of surprise is important to the success of our venture.*'

I was surprised alright, who wouldn't be? Beefy great man coming straight at me. Anything could've happened. Our Sandra was hopping mad, made me promise to write and complain, but before I could put pen to paper, another letter arrives. At least they got my name right this time.

'Dear Mrs Mathison,

There appears to have been some kind of an error. We were expecting you in Pembroke Street on Monday last, not Tuesday. Our records indicate.....

I could hardly believe my eyes. No apology, no explanation, just a bill for £125.

I'd had someone else's accident!

Sisters under the Skin

It came as a shock, I can tell you, to find that my little foibles, those things which I assumed make me uniquely bonkers, where not mine and mine alone. I was reading this Irish author – the one who writes with such a strong brogue it hurls itself off the page to box your ears – and I was having to read very slowly, so the narrator in my head could do justice to it.

I thought I'd bought a novel, to keep me amused while I was waiting, but I'll come to that later. It was one of those airport special offers too good to miss, except now I have to carry them as well as the holiday selection already sitting like lead in the hand luggage. Anyhow, I was wrong. Not a novel at all, but the confessions of..... well..... an obsessive. And I just knew we were going to get along.

Shoes, let's start with shoes. There's a whole monologue devoted to them, and many passing references. She scours the globe in search of the perfect pair, the exact match for the handbag. Or the other way round, she's not much bothered which comes first. She loves the thrill of it. But the quest for shoes, in my experience, is not without anxiety. There's the worry that your big toe might have poked a hole through your tights and will emerge, to your shame, slightly blue–tinged and strangled in a rim of nylon. Worse still, the summer heat. Let's just say that shoe shopping should be done first thing, before the feet get into their stride.

Of course, there's nothing wrong with a passion for shoes, although Imelda's was probably over the top. No, the planning of every outfit should begin at the feet. And I practice what I preach. Even your most basic footwear collection needs at least seven pairs. There's the plain court, allowing an acceptable walking speed when in a rush, while still adding height if there's a need to be assertive. These will last through spring and autumn and be replaced in summer by the sling back variety or, on really hot days, strap–happy sandals. Winter demands a little more protection in the shape of boots. Knee length for outdoors, the shorter, ankle length version for indoors and smart gatherings. Then there are the FMs – high heeled, tarty and almost impossible to walk in but they make your legs look fabulous and, hey, who needs to walk. Add to the list a pair of cool flip–flops and there's your seven. That's before taking colour, comfort and any sporting tendencies into consideration.

This goes to explain the weight of the suitcase.

Now, I have to come clean here. Apart from the books and the shoes, it's my toilet bag that tips me into the excess baggage charge. I'm a hoarder of lotions and potions, you see, many of which travel with me – the cosmetic equivalent of a security blanket – and

I could never resist a bargain. It's the lure of that extra purchase which secures, for very little additional outlay, the designer holdall stuffed full of samples. It matters not that they're not your colour, or might provoke an allergic reaction.

But even Salinger's bathroom cabinet couldn't compete with hers. Plus she'd filled drawers, chests, carrier bags and possibly that chunky, see–through under–bed storage as well. She's got products I've never heard of, let alone know what to do with.

How long, I wonder, would it take me to get out of the house with just some of it? Cleanse, tone, moisturise. Fair enough. Five minutes, say, for a really thorough job. Then blot, to get rid of the shine. Hide those dark circles with dots of concealer; apply foundation, not forgetting the neck. Blot again, or your collars will match your face. Probably ten minutes gone by now and cheeks, lips and eyes are still naked. Forget it, life's too short. A quick lick of mascara will have to do; one minute at most. Unless, that is, I poke myself in the eye.

We are, however, completely in accord, on the subject of fake tan. While, like her, I would prefer the real thing, these days my shins will simply not surrender their pallor. And I no longer have the patience for spit roasting. I do think she should read the instructions more carefully, though. I never end up with orange palms. Well, perhaps just a hint of a tint in between the fingers.

Lists. How we love them. Things to do, things to buy, letters to write, books to read – the possibilities are endless. We employ the same trick, she and I, starting with things we've already done. It's so satisfying when you cross them off.

Nowadays I make my lists in a book – which will probably be worthy of publication one day – where they won't go astray. Imagine the trauma of a day adrift, or a stranger glimpsing your private life. 'Tits and teeth' were on one of mine, shorthand reminders of the day's appointments. I suspect it got wrapped with a Christmas present but nobody said. I missed them both and had to wait months.

Which brings me back to waiting, the story of my life, my curriculum vitae. Have I mentioned my loathing for lateness, my own included? Add to that a useless sense of direction and the upshot is I'm always early. I must've spent days, if not weeks, hanging about – for friends to turn up, my interview slot, the flight to be called. Take today, for instance, I had four hours in hand, that's before any 'terminal' delays. One disadvantage is the volume of coffee – this is my third – which sends me twitching about my business. On the plus side, though, I've got through my list. Even the pair of pink Ferragamos she'd give her eye teeth for. But it's hard on the feet all that shopping – I'll be glad of those shoes in the hand luggage later – and the constant need to check the screens.

Speaking of which, they've announced my gate. Must run........

A tribute to Marian Keyes.

Fast and Lose

"Welcome to you all and thanks for turning out on such a nasty night. I know how hard it can be to leave a cosy sofa in front of the telly – but you won't regret it, not one bit!" The stick thin woman standing at the front calls the room to order with an acid–sharp voice.

Wendy and Sheila creep in the back, trying to be unobtrusive, but she looks up and spots them.

"Come on in, don't be shy. No, no you're not late. What's a few minutes between friends." She guffaws. "There are some seats free over there, by the window."

They move along the row trying not to tread on toes. But there isn't much room and neither is what you might call petite.

"Pooh, it smells odd in here." Wendy pinches her nose.

"That'll be the feet."

"What?"

"Or the rubber."

"Rubber!!"

"Yes, plimsoles, mats and things. This is used as a gym as well as for assemblies." Sheila teaches in this very school.

"Oh, nice. Don't the windows open?"

"Is there a problem over there? We can't be wasting time, you know. Time is money, as they say."

"Oops, Sticklady strikes. Not much gets past her." Wendy giggles and nudges Sheila's ribs.

"Stoppit. You'll get us thrown out," she snorts.

"Right. First things first. You need to register yourselves as part of the group and pay your subscription. £10 for the first meeting, that's inclusive of the registration fee. Subsequent meetings cost a mere £6. Very reasonable, I'm sure you'll agree." She gives them her best treacly smile.

"How many here?" Wendy asks behind her hand.

Sheila does a quick calculation. "About 30 I'd say."

"Pretty good takings for a couple of hours work."

Wendy takes the register coming along their row. "She wants name, address and 'phone number. Do you think we should?"

"I expect it's all right. Hang on, I'll check." Sheila raises her hand.

"Yes?" Sticklady is still smiling.

"I was just wondering, are we covered, you know, for Data Protection and all that. I mean, these are personal details." Sheila teaches computer studies.

"Absolutely. My associate," she flaps a hand in vague introduction, "deals with that side of things but I can assure you that we are well up on the legalities. Nothing to worry about at all. Now, if you'll pass the register and the cash box to the last row we can get on with the business in hand."

"Is it my imagination or did that smile just slip?" Wendy passes the box over her shoulder.

"Could be."

"Ladies. Oh do excuse me, and gentleman. May I say how very nice it is to have a man amongst us. One who clearly cares about his health and appearance." More treacle.

"You have embarked upon an adventure tonight, and one which will change your lives. For why else are we all here? How many of you are sick and tired of those diets, searching for the one that will work for you? I knew it – just look at that show of hands. Well your search ends here. And I am the living proof."

"I suppose she is alive?" Sheila whispers. "If she turns sideways she'll vanish."

"That might be the only way to stop her." Wendy moans.

But Sticklady is in her stride.

"Now what is this miracle I'm about to offer you? I can feel your anticipation so I won't make you wait a moment longer." She pauses............enjoying the moment.

"Fasting," she screeches and flings her arms wide in enthusiasm.

There is complete hush.

"Yes, I know. Fantastic isn't it?"

Stunned silence. A hand goes up in the second row. "Um, I'm not sure......you did say fasting? You mean not eating?"

"Absolutely."

"What no food at all?"

"Cor–rect."

A mumble spreads through the hall like a rumour. Glances are passing back and forth.

"Well, I think it's wonderful." A lime green shell–suited woman leaps to her feet. "And so simple."

"She's the one who's simple." Wendy whispers in disbelief.

"Either that or she's the associate, the one who's..... 'well up on the legalities'," Sheila mimics.

"There ought to be a law against that colour." Wendy laughs sliding down in her seat to avoid detection. "Uh–oh, now she's asking for trouble." Wendy points to a rotund woman two rows ahead. "Too late."

"You." All eyes follow the accusing finger. "Yes you there in the cardigan. Are you eating?"

Caught in the act and blushing to the roots of her curly perm, the woman tries to swallow. "Erm mon mway frm....."

"Unbelievable. Why is it you're here? As if we couldn't tell. I suggest you get your priorities right, now who's next?"

"So how long do we do this fasting?" Another daring weight watcher enters the fray.

"For as long as it takes, of course." The gleam in Sticklady's eye is hardening. "What did you think, that it'd be easy? If that were the case you'd already be thin."

Gasps replace the mumble. A forest of hands shoots up.

"What about exercise, won't we be too weak?"

"Exercise? – nasty sweaty business. We don't believe in it. You can all do without those ugly bulgy muscles. Now, just one more then we must get on, yes, you there in the anorak."

"But isn't it dangerous?"

"Dangerous? How can it be dangerous, are you mad? It's been tried and tested all over the world. And people pay a lot more than you have, let me tell you, to be starved at a health spa or some ashram." Her voice rises an octave.

"With respect, I think ...."

"Respect!" Shrill now. "Don't talk to me of respect. Am I not the expert here? And what do I get?... questions, questions, questions." Another octave. "For goodness sake, fasting plays a part in many religions. Can all those millions be wrong?"

"Madam!" Mr Gilbert stands, outraged. "It is you who are wrong." He collects his dignity and walks out. A lime green streak runs after him.

"Told you." Sheila's enjoying herself.

Sticklady is losing control.

"Excuse me." A tentative arm is raised. "I presume we can drink."

"Well what do you think?" dripping sarcasm. She shakes her head in disbelief. "I'm dealing with imbeciles and ignoramuses. Or should that be that ignorami? Oh who gives a damn?" muttering to herself. "For God's......." but pulls herself together. Best not enter the realms of blasphemy. "Even Jesus was allowed a drink."

"That's done it." Wendy flinches as chairs scrape the floor.

Sticklady stands before her audience astounded. "Hold on. Where do you think you're going? You've made a commitment, you won't get your money back." This has never happened to her before. "What's the matter with you? Can't face it huh? A teeny weeny taste of discomfort? No, I thought not. You want to be fatties all your lives.........your flabby, miserable lives."

"How did we get caught up in that? The woman's a nutter." Wendy links arms with Sheila now they can no longer hear the screaming. "She reminds me of that cult, what were they called, the airyfairyans or something. They starved themselves to death." She stops suddenly, looks down and smiles at what she sees. "Still, hardly likely here?" They laugh. "'Fast to Lose' it said. Seemed innocent enough."

"Actually," the penny drops. "it was 'Fast *and* Lose', now I come to think of it. Conned by a conjunction." Sheila also teaches English. "I didn't put in my £10, by the way, did you?"

"Certainly not," Wendy giggles. "Fancy a drink?"

The Body Shop

"You'll look after your Gran, won't you?"

"Course I will."

"Go out with her, take her shopping. She loves shopping?"

"Of course."

"Thanks my lovely. I knew I could count on you."

My Gran smiles over her spoon, which is loaded with whipped cream and poised between her cup and lips.

"Low fat cream this." One of her trademark twinkles accompanies the next smile, then her spoon plunges for another attack.

She also loves Starbucks, and we're working our way through the menu. Today I'm having a double-shot vanilla cappuccino, Gran has chosen a towering concoction which promises mind-blowing mocha somewhere beneath the cream. I have my doubts, but Gran is tucking in.

It's no hardship for me to keep my promise to Granddad. I've always had a good time with my Gran. When I was little we used to go off on adventures; she'd show me the cowslips growing on the common, take me along the river looking for kingfishers. Once we caught the train to Brighton to see the pier.

Now, years later, we still meet when we can, for what she calls 'our little outings'. Expeditions more like. She collects me in her car and whizzes me off to some town or other. We always start with coffee, after the excitement of parking, that is. Gran can squeeze her Polo into the smallest space. Then we catch up with our news and plan the day. There'll be lunch, perhaps a visit to a gallery or museum afterwards, especially if there's something new on display, and shopping. Plenty of shopping. Bath has a lot to offer.

While we finish our coffee, I sneak a peek or two at her, check she's all right. Today she looks more whacky than usual. She's been at the low lights again – they look pretty good in her newly cropped hair – and she's wearing blue jeans. They look good too. She's not slim, my Gran. Robust, that's how she thinks of herself. Substantial.

"Your Granddad liked a woman he could get hold of," she told me once, "and he knew I wouldn't snap when he gave me a hug."

She has cleverly concealed any lumps and bumps with an enormous asymmetric sweater the colour of a Scottish heath – bracken, and peat with a hint of sky. Her skin has that outdoor glow too, enhanced by a touch of blusher. The lipstick is sure to be a matching tone, except it's vanished under a layer of frothy cream. She's doing fine.

"Have you heard the one about......."

She laughs like a drain as she gets to the end of the joke about the Englishman, the American and the Japanese stranded in the woods. We never reach the punch line, she's laughing so much, then so am I, can't help myself. She gets most of her jokes from a young Dane in her evening class. With his aptitude for mistranslation, and her readiness to roar at anything, I doubt they get to the punch lines either.

We pull ourselves together, dabbing gently at the corners of our eyes to prevent a trickle of mascara–tinted tears.

"D'you fancy this?" She pushes a brochure across the table. Two very large, fur–coated women of a certain age adorn the front cover. 'Cruising for Toy Boys' it's called, and they're clearly determined. I raise an eyebrow.

"Not the 'cruising', although......" there's that twinkle again. "The exhibition. Beryl Cook. It's just round the corner."

We have our lunch beside the river in a small Pizzeria. Gran loves Italian food and says the pizza here is good, almost as good as she tasted in Gubbio, that split-level town where cable cars dangle precariously from wires connecting the two. We take our time choosing, persuading the chef to adapt his special with our favourite toppings – artichoke hearts, capers and olives. Prompted by our surroundings, I'm treated to one of her Italian holiday stories while we wait. She and my Granddad travelled a lot.

We usually stick to one glass of wine but Gran opts for a second. She's rosy–cheeked when we leave.

"Shops first, I think. Anything you need?" She slips her arm through mine

"Nothing much. How about you?"

"Just one or two things from The Body Shop."

"Now there's a surprise." I give her arm a squeeze.

We wander through the smaller streets, peering into boutiques, luggage shops, cheese makers. We forego tea in the Pump Room, Gran thinks they make it with the spa water. Before long we approach our target, the unmistakable smell greets us and Gran is among the lotions and potions in a trice.

"Lily milk soap, have you got it?"

The assistant doesn't think so, can't remember it.

"It was wonderful. Rich red, like that chocolate covered Turkish Delight, and the smell," Gran pauses, "sandalwood, musk, lily of course, and something else. You really should stock it again."

We drift along, lifting bottles and jars from the glass shelves, sniffing, dabbing, comparing, then replacing them.

"The packaging's so simple." Gran has hold of a plastic, black capped bottle she's brought with her. She hands it across the counter for a top–up of shampoo. "Keeps the price down, less waste. Good idea, isn't it?"

I pick up a pot of eye gel and some glitzy nail scrub. Gran's basket is almost full when we join the queue.

"Look at this lot. I can't resist. Your Granddad was always teasing me. Said he'd sprinkle my ashes here when the time came, my own personal heaven." She slips her credit card back into her purse. "Right then, let's go and find Beryl."

Gran's death surprised us all. She'd kept it to herself, her heart condition.

Her ashes, most of them anyway, sit in an urn beside Granddad's on the mantle shelf. It took just a couple of scoops to fill the black–capped bottle and faking the label was easy enough. I took it to her local branch, placed it high up on the 'For Display Only' shelf, where it doesn't look grey at all. It sparkles, lavishly reflecting colour from the crystals and oils all around. Gran's paradise.

Inspired by Beryl Cook, and her husband's playful promise to sprinkle her ashes in her favourite shop which, incidentally, is not this one.

The Other Royale Wedding

The red Dodge pickup looked fantastic; parked outside St Matthew's, her paintwork sparkling, chrome trim gleaming. Ribbons attached to the battery of searchlights atop her cab streamed across the flatbed. The posy of cream roses and freesia in the centre of her grille was beautiful, elegant.

Betty Royale, that's Royal with an 'e', – she was determined to be spelt correctly – stepped out of husband Alf's Volvo. As mother of the bride she thought, and not for the first time, what a strange way for her daughter to arrive. Alf went off to park at the rear of the church. Betty waited at the lych gate smiling as the guests arrived.

Poppy wanted to get there first. She had driven herself, determined to park the pickup right outside, in pride of place. Betty couldn't dissuade her.

"It's not done, love. You're supposed to arrive once we're all assembled, make an entrance."

They'd compromised. Poppy would wait in the grounds. Dave, her soon–to–be husband would arrive on his Harley, best man riding pillion. Betty sighed, and tried to look cheerful.

Alf joined Betty at the gate to greet the last of the guests. Betty, nerves beginning to show, brushed at non–existent specks on his jacket. She straightened his tie, also unnecessary.

"Stop fiddling, love. I'll do as I am, won't I?"

"You will, Alf. You will. She gave him one of her bear hugs. "Now, go and fetch your daughter. It's almost time."

He found her among the headstones, as he knew he would, talking to her Gran. He felt his chest swell at the sight of her, as always, but today he thought he could burst with pride. Curtains of gleaming red hair hid her expression as she bent forward, but he knew she'd have that solemn look on her face as she laid her bouquet on the grave.

He waited till she stood.

"I wanted her to have it before the wedding, Dad, so it's just between her and me."

"I know. She'd have come round in the end, love. You always were her favourite." He paused. "Right then, are we ready?"

The size of her grin told him all he needed to know.

They walked up the aisle to the nasal twang of 'Stand by Your Man'. The cuban heels of her white cowgirl boots, almost hidden beneath the lace, marked time with the beat. Alf felt himself growing taller as the congregation turned to smile at them. He handed her to Dave – he would never think of it as giving her away – and slipped into his pew. Betty, already shiny–eyed, gave his arm a squeeze, then reached in her bag for a fresh tissue.

The service was beautiful. Betty was entranced, committed every detail to memory, ready for entertaining her friends. She was secretly pleased the 'other' Royal Wedding had been put off to today, it would add a little extra something to the telling. She did sigh quietly, though, as they left the church to Dolly Parton promising always to love you–oo–oo, thinking a bit of Mendelssohn would've been nice. But as she followed Poppy and Dave down the aisle she had no doubt they were made for one another.

Dave hoisted a giggling Poppy into the pickup and jumped into the driving seat. Cascades of real rose petals, Betty's idea, swirled around as they headed off.

Alf stood with the vicar while the guests mulled around, catching up on family news and arranging lifts to the reception, then went to fetch the Volvo.

Betty was accompanied down the gravel path by the best man and two of the ushers. What a strange mixture, Alf thought, as he rounded the corner from the car park and saw them – Middle England meets Memphis. And he had to smile when he noticed how the red of Betty's hat exactly matched the bootlace ties the lads were wearing. And her suit was the self–same silver–grey as their knee–length jackets. Just like they belonged together.

Flight of Fancy

For Ted – no ordinary airman

The pilot strode towards me across the grubby linoleum.

"Mr Edwards? I'm Jim Scott."

He tugged at his gloves and offered his hand. It was cold despite having been wrapped in leather.

"So sorry to be late. I hope you haven't been waiting long."

"Only 63 years." That stopped him in his tracks all right.

"Well then, I'll have to make sure you're not disappointed."

We were in the flying school HQ, a tatty shed of a building with a corrugated roof, scruffy furniture, and draughts.

Jim led us to the window. "There she is."

A small swoop of excitement unsteadied me for a second. There she was indeed. A bright yellow Tiger Moth, holding her own out there among the twin engines and the single seaters. I could hardly wait to get at her.

It took a few minutes to get me kitted out in a brown all–in–one flying suit topped with a sheepskin–lined bomber jacket. One whiff of the leather and I was back there – 1940, Inverness, pilot training. The cigarette smoke, thick as fog; the laughter, at nothing much and getting louder as flying time drew near. I read somewhere that parachute jumpers reach maximum stress 20 minutes before the jump. Then their training takes over and the tension eases, cool and professional, ready for action. I reckon that goes for pilots too. There was always a hush before take off.

I followed Jim out of the shed. I was glad of the gear once we were outside, a cold northerly had sprung up. The Tiger was parked just the other side of the security gate, no chocks against her wheels. We'd've been on a charge for that in the mob, leaving a Tiger on the loose.

Jim pulled on his helmet and tested the radio. "Send out a winder, soon as you can. Right, Mr Edwards, I'll take the rear position, you climb up front."

To be honest, I wondered if I'd be able to, but once I took hold of the wing struts I knew what to do, where to tread. And the thrill of it put a spring into my old knees.

"Stand on the seat, then lower yourself in."

Jim strapped me in and helped me with my helmet.

As I adjusted the earphones I could swear I heard my old instructor.

"Nose up, speed down. Nose down, speed up. And what we want is level lad, right? Straight and bloody level."

'Picka', we called him, 'cos his name was Field. And it was good advice in an emergency!

While we settled ourselves into the cockpit, and checked we could talk to one another, Tom arrived with the chocks and kicked them against the wheels.

"Get that elastic wound up nice and tight," I told him.

"Yours a forty minute flight?"

"It is."

"OK. I'll give it 120 turns." That made us laugh. Then they got serious.

It can be a dangerous business, starting a prop. Heavy great things they are, and spin at a fair old lick once you get them going. I saw a lad get hit by one. Don't know what made him turn the wrong way. His injuries were terrible.

Jim and Tom went by the book. With the power switched off, Tom gave the prop a few turns, forcing some petrol into the pistons, priming the engine. Then he stepped back.

"Switch on," he called.

Jim reached for the switch on the side of the cockpit.

"Switch on," he repeated, indicating with a thumb up.

Tom grabbed the blade with his left hand, swung it sharply downwards then turned immediately to his right, walking away, keeping clear. No spark, the engine didn't turn over.

"Switch off."

"Switch off." Jim's thumb pointed down and Tom approached for another try.

A couple more goes then she caught with that throaty de Havilland growl, and we were bumping and rattling across the grass.

The Tiger doesn't need a runway, not as such. Point her into the wind, open the throttle and she'll be up before you know it. And with little weight to hold her down she lifts fast and easy. I felt that familiar buzz as up we went.

"Ready to take the controls?" Jim levelled her.

"Sure," I said with much more confidence than I felt.

It wasn't like riding a bike, I can tell you that. It didn't all come flooding back. Of course I knew what had to be done, I'd clocked up 72 hours in Tigers, before graduating to Wellingtons and Liberators. Doing it was another matter. And the old girl wasn't exactly at her best. The altimeter was working, but she had no artificial horizon, so I needed to fix on the real one. Trouble was, a dark circle of cloud sitting above us like a lid was squeezing a blinding red rim out at its edges. The horizon was ablaze. Flying level was tricky.

Flying straight was harder than it should've been too. It brought to mind my first solo. Four and three–quarter hours instruction under my belt, they needed us up fast in those days, and I was almost sick with fear.

"Take her up again Edwards, do a few circuits. And don't break anything."

I taxied across the airfield, running through the checklists, sweating inside my suit. My heart was pounding so hard I didn't hear the tower.

"Have you gone deaf, Edwards?" The shout got my attention. "Get that plane in the air."

The takeoff was a bumpy affair. I banked too steeply and my stomach hit my throat. I corrected, overcorrected but finally got her level. I lurched into a dive, pulled her up, nearly stalled. Then suddenly, it was easy, automatic. Like the plane had become part of me. I was flying.

"She needs a little right rudder," Jim came to the rescue, "the turn and bank indicator is permanently offset. And the airspeed indicator's stuck at fifty knots. But that shouldn't bother and old hand like you." He chuckled down the microphone.

We chatted amiably for the rest of the flight, Jim pointing out landmarks, gently putting me right when I needed it. As we turned to join the circuit towards the end of my forty minutes, the sun broke through. I was blinded for a moment by a shaft of light reflected from the lake on my left.

Coastal Command. Two Wellingtons patrolling a sector, I'm flying the second. We're just about to turn for home at the end of our stint when we see them, German flakboats. The Four Horsemen we call them. They skulk about off the Dutch coast, slow enough to trick the radar, heavily armed and lying in wait. We get our orders. Attack!

Snorkel leaves his charts, moves to bomb–aiming position. The old Wimpey doesn't have much in the way of guns so we need to fly past and drop our load. Wally, in front, goes into his dive. We hold fire, waiting.... waiting. Come on Wally turn, pull up. Bullets rip through the fuselage above my head, tear into the wing. We smell the fuel.

I squeeze my eyes against the glare. And the memory.

"We're cleared for landing." Jim lined up with the runway, eased back on the throttle then lifted the nose just before touch down.

"I've not had many like that," I told him. "a perfect three point landing."

"Thanks," he said, then added with affection, "there's no other way to treat a lady."

All Stitched Up

The knife sliced into the flesh of her thumb. Blood seeped into the creamy flesh of the courgette, spreading a watery red stain.

"That's what you get for watching TV with a knife in your hand!" Kate stared, fascinated, as the colour darkened, then sucked at the swelling bead. "Not exactly life–threatening."

Used to these one–way conversations, she continued chopping vegetables just managing to resist the urge to arrange them according to colour, like the servant girl in that novel about Vermeer. She could see the appeal though. Colour was Kate's passion.

Her mind drifted, assigning attributes. Blood red, powerful. Lemon yellow, sharp, made her mouth water just thinking about it. Black, velvet–smooth, sinister. Kate opted for sinister.

The telephone rang making her jump. Chunks of carrot and pepper scattered.

"Darling, hi. Sorry but I'm going to be late."

"No, not again."

"What's that noise?" he interrupted.

"Just the TV."

"This early! That's not like you. Anyway, I need a few hours to get this project sewn up. Back by 9 at the latest. Okay?"

She stood for a second receiver in hand, thoughts of the sinister filling her head, then dialled.

"Sadie, hi, it's Kate. Fancy a drink?"

They met at seven in a favourite wine bar. One of several they'd adopted since discovering that both husbands were totally addicted to work.

"Got another new project has he?" Sadie put down two glasses of chilled white.

"No. Finishing an old one. Tom reckons a big effort now means he can come to Boston next week."

"He's actually taking time off?"

"You're joking." Resignation tainted Kate's laugh. "He'll still be working, just in a different place."

"Mark's the same. I'm beginning to think his laptop's grafted on. Do you sometimes wonder why we bother?"

"Yes, often."

Sadie looked up, checking to see if Kate had meant it.

"Well, you know, in those idle moments. But the strands of our lives are so intertwined. Just like my tapestry threads when the dog's been among them." Kate laughed. "What a mess he makes."

"Speaking of which," Sadie was relieved by the change of subject, "how's that business of yours coming along?"

"Pretty well."

Kate had given up her job to pursue a new career. Years with a busy graphic design firm had left her with an aching neck, worn out and more than a little cynical. She was in demand, especially for her stunning blends of colour. She'd been encouraged to experiment, but within limits, which left her disappointed and tied down. Then a particularly hostile takeover meant too many people after too few jobs. Kate was quick to join the queue for redundancy, and freedom.

Three years on her tapestries were selling well. To her trademark use of colour she'd added texture, using fine silks, richly dyed wools and metallic threads. The designs were sensational, the sewing simple, well within the reach of the unskilled enthusiast.

"I'm quite surprised to tell the truth." Kate went on. "Of course my weirdest designs took some time, but they're selling now, here and abroad."

"The trip to Boston. Well done you." Sadie raised her glass. "I find those weird ones a bit spooky actually."

"They're meant to be. There are layers in the design, concealing and revealing. You have to look at them differently, sort of sideways, to see it all."

She had found a way to build images, one on top of another, so they became not quite themselves. And the colours appeared to shift of their own accord.

"But it's not just the colours." Sadie searched for words. "There's something eerie lurking, just out of reach. I can't quite explain."

"Oh I know exactly." A faraway look passed across Kate's face. "Like fairy tales."

Sadie's surprise was obvious. "You mean Cinderella and Little Red Riding Hood? Happy ever after and all that?"

"Not those, no. The nasty ones. Haven't you noticed there's always something lurking, a wicked stepmother, a snow queen, a pricked finger? Things are never quite as they seem. That's what I'm aiming for."

"Bullseye, I'd say."

"Thanks. Another drink?"

"Why not?"

Summer slipped into autumn. Days shortened as the sun dropped more rapidly. Kate stood at her studio window watching the spectacle.

"Beautiful, isn't it?" Tom came and stood beside her to watch it too. A gash of red tore through the inky, blue–black cloud, spreading to leave purple and magenta in its wake.

"Looks like a wound. The sky's bleeding."

"What?" Startled, Tom stared at her. "That's a bit gory, sweetheart. Are you okay?"

"Mmm. Yes. Fine thanks."

"Those fairy tales must be getting to you."

Kate smiled, but didn't reply.

With autumn in full swing trees shifted into their evening dress – warm, rich colours – full of promise. Then, with a kind of mockery, they stripped to reveal themselves, stark, dark, and foreboding. Kate walked miles with her dog, nourished by the atmosphere. Brooding, she gave free reign to her imagination; the dog ecstatic, scenting prey both real and invented, charging off in pursuit. Hours passed, a design was taking shape.

Today the river brooded too, sliding miserably between muddy banks swallowing reflections into khaki–green depths.

"A secretive colour," she thought. "Perfect to hide in, or to trap the unsuspecting."

The dog pranced about on the bank ready to retrieve the ball she always launched. But she was suddenly uneasy.

"Not today, Timbo." She had the oddest feeling that the river might swallow him too. Calling him to heel she turned for home, coloured thoughts painting pictures in her head.

"We're back." Kate called up the stairs, draping her coat across the banister.

No answer but the tapping keys told her Tom was home.

"Do you want coffee?"

"Not now. I'm a bit tied up."

"Sadie and Mark'll be here at eight. Remember?"

"Dammit, I forgot. I really want to get this finished."

"Can't put them off now. Eight o'clock. Okay?"

Kate took coffee into her studio. A design was slowly taking shape in her head. Pulling open the narrow drawers which held her threads, she selected several and moved across to her desk. Slowly she began arranging the colours, starting with the greens.

"These cushions are fantastic." Sadie was impressed. "I haven't seen them before."

"No. They're part of the new range."

"Do you make them yourself?" Mark picked up a cushion, trying to estimate how long it would take. "There must be hundreds of stitches."

"Thousands actually. And no, I don't stitch them all, just the original. I sell the design."

"Fortunately." Tom added, sipping his gin. "I bought her the first kit years ago, thought it would be relaxing."

Kate took up the tale. "It drove me insane, poking the needle in and out. Once I got so angry I stabbed myself. You can still see the scar." Kate held up her palm. "Bled all over the canvas. I needed dark colours to cover the stain."

"Not this one I hope?" Mark grimaced, putting down the cushion.

"On that gory note let's go through and eat. After

you, ladies." Tom waited for Mark. "I was hoping to pick your brains about a problem at work."

Sadie caught Kate's eye, and shrugged.

The following week Kate visited her supplier, always a pleasure. The shop was tucked away in a tiny village and looked like a dolls' house. A single step took Kate into another world. The walls were alive with every shade and hue. Threads, nets, velvets, beads, ribbons; cottons piled high and spilling everywhere. Needles shining sharp, scissors exotic or surgical; wooden frames displaying works in progress or complete. Delicious as the inside of the gingerbread house. She loved it all.

"Hello, Kate dear. Good to see you. How can we help today?"

Rebecca came down the rickety ladder from the loft with surprising ease. She and her sister had owned and run the shop for years. They were always ready to help, their knowledge of stitchery second to none, and were delighted to demonstrate their skill, despite fingers gnarled with age.

"Good to see you too. I've brought a new design." Kate unfurled the canvas spreading it on the counter.

"Going through a green period are we?" chuckled Rebecca. "Ah, and it's not revealing its secret yet."

"No, not yet." Kate turned to scan the racks. "I'm looking for something dense, matt, that absorbs the light."

"A darker shade here perhaps?" Rebecca leant over

the canvas, twisting a light for a better view.

"No, not there. That green is exactly right."

Rebecca moved closer. "What are these white flecks, mixed in the background?"

Kate leant forward too, and laughed, tugging gently at the hairs. "That, Rebecca, is dog hair. Timbo's been snuggling in the wool."

"There's an old tale, you know, about hair woven into tapestry. The weaver holds the power to grant a wish, if it was added accidentally."

"Old Timbo gets an extra walk then." Kate's voice quietened. "What about spilled blood?"

Rebecca looked up sharply. "That's a different matter altogether, much more sinister some would have us believe. And not one to meddle with." A shiver ran through her and she looked closely at Kate. "Let's get back to the thread, shall we? Take a look at this chenille. I've a feeling it might be just the thing."

The next few weeks saw Kate in a fever of stitching, unpicking and restitching until colour and texture produced the exact effect. The chenille was perfect, adding a dense, velvety layer to the canvas, subtly shifting, concealing and revealing. She spent more time in her studio, seemed distracted. Even Tom began to notice.

"Still at it I see." Tom came to stand behind her one evening, peering over her shoulder. "Your fingers'll be raw at this rate."

Kate put the canvas down, covering it with a cloth, and showed him her hands. "Not yet."

"Another wound though." She didn't reply, just picked at the plaster on her finger. "I expect I'll come in here one day and you'll buried under a mound of cushions."

"Or vanished altogether," she thought.

It was finished at last and Kate was delighted. Despite false starts and a deal of frustration the end result was worth it, made a fabulous cushion. Not for sale, though. This one was to keep. And she knew exactly where it should go.

Tom stretched, arms high above his head. He'd solved it, finally. The hours it had taken had been no joking matter. He'd worked day and night. Now he was extremely pleased with himself, and more than a little relieved. He stood up and stretched again, flexing his back, glad to move away from his desk, then he went in search of Kate and a drink of something cool and intoxicating.

"Kate, d'you want a drink?" Tom wandered down the stairs and into the kitchen, poured two glasses of Chablis from the bottle in the fridge and headed for her studio, disappointed not to find her. The house always felt odd when Kate wasn't there. Quiet and empty.

He drifted into the living room, glad the fire was lit, not for the warmth but for comfort. As he set Kate's drink down on the glass–topped table he noticed the cushion. It was large, covering almost the whole back of her chair. Bigger than any of the others she'd made. And the colours were extraordinary. Shades of green, at least he thought they were, and something very dark. But they seemed to shift as he looked, come alive almost.

"Must be the fire," he thought, "flickering life into the design."

He moved closer, trying to decipher it. He picked it up for a better view. Then put it back, moved away, perched on the chair opposite and stared. He took a sip of wine then settled back, letting the deep feather padding draw him in. So comfortable and warm he would be asleep before long. He drained his glass and stretched out his legs, crossing them loosely at the ankles. Finally, with an elbow supported by the arm of the chair, he nestled his chin into a cupped palm. In that delicious moment before drifting into sleep he knew.......

It was him. A picture of Tom, in that very chair. The likeness was uncanny. The clothes were the same, almost merging with the khaki–green background. The image slipped in and out of focus while Tom struggled against a sudden weariness. He sagged, eyelids heavy, sank deeper into the chair. Flames burst briefly through the coals, lighting the room. For a second the image on the cushion flared. Then it disappeared.

And so did Tom.

Kate and Timbo walked alongside the river, as it slid khaki–green and brooding between muddy banks.

"Ready boy?" Kate hurled the ball. She was happy to let him swim today.

Pat White was an Executive Director of the Oxford Radcliffe Hospitals NHS Trust until taking early retirement in 1999. She has been writing ever since.

Neil Drury comes from a background of children's book publishing but now works as an artist, illustrator and art teacher, in and around Oxfordshire.